I0564095

IN THE DEVIL'S CRADLE

Other Books by S. L. Edwards

Whiskey and Other Unusual Ghosts
The Death of An Author

Praise for S. L. Edwards's *In the Devil's Cradle*

"In the Devil's Cradle is rich, sweepingly grand in the manner of the best historical fiction, and haunting in its detail of lives caught up in the machinery of political change. A fine, assured debut by Edwards that has me looking forward to more."

—Laird Barron, author of *Swift to Chase*

"*In the Devil's Cradle* has a family at its core, but it's not so much a question of them being haunted by something from their past as them being pursued by the dark spirit of a nation that has an affinity for their souls. A deft look at the political dimensions of the supernatural, and the investments of different factions to keep something alive that may well be better off dead."

—Brian Evenson, author of *Song for the Unraveling of the World*

"In the Devil's Cradle is the political gothic horror I didn't know I needed in my life, and I'm here for it. This book oozes dread and suspense, with a central mystery reminiscent of Machen's work. An enthralling debut."

—Todd Keisling, author of *Devil's Creek*

"Edwards combines an intelligent literary sensibility with a deep appreciation for the supernatural and its purpose in our lives. He creates fascinating stories that consider both the vulnerability and the possibilities contained in the human condition. If you want speculative fiction with great heart, distinctive prose, and a strong sense of history, you will find it here."

—S.P . Miskowski, author of *I Wish I Was Like You*

"With *In the Devil's Cradle* S. L. Edwards has written a masterpiece, a gothic tale equal parts Marquez and Poe, of a haunted house writ large, where the house is a nation, and the ghosts are the legends and lies and secrets that haunt its citizenry, sometimes with tenderness, and sometimes with brutality, and where the phantasmagorical wander the streets and forests imprisoned in chains of dread memories and forgotten sacrifices."

—Peter Rawlik, author of *The Weird Company*

Praise for S. L. Edwards's *In the Devil's Cradle* (continued)

"…the real horror of this novel is that Antioch could be any country, and the terrors both real and supernatural could easily be set loose upon us all. A chilling story that holds appeal for a wide audience, but especially for fans of *The Hacienda*, by Isabel Cañas (2022), *Frankenstein in Baghdad*, by Ahmed Saadawi (2018), and *Wonderland*, by Zoje Stage (2020)."
—Becky Spratford, *Booklist*

"The bones of this story are unearthed from several horror traditions. Edwards often uses classic tropes to tell his stories, which in my mind, gives credence to the idea of horror, the genre, as a language beyond anything else. There are many ways to tell the story of a nation in crisis, but Edwards uses the vocabulary of ghost stories, folk horror, and gothic fiction to craft something sinister and acutely recognizable."
—Carson Winter, author of *Bloodlines: Four Tales of Familial Fear*

IN THE DEVIL'S CRADLE

S. L. EDWARDS

WORD HORDE
PETALUMA, CA

In the Devil's Cradle © 2022 by S. L. Edwards
This edition of *In the Devil's Cradle* © 2022 by Word Horde

Cover art and design © 2022 by Yves Tourigny

Edited by Ross E. Lockhart

All rights reserved

First Edition

ISBN: 978-1-956252-03-3

A Word Horde Book
www.wordhorde.com

For my grandmama, who gave me all the family's stories.

*T*he story of a nation begins with a woman's ragged breath. It starts running, with scraped, bleeding feet and a child she holds tight to her chest. It's recited through her blinking, searing tears and told in her dry, raspy screams.

The story of a nation pursues her relentlessly. It hounds her through the forests, across the rivers, through the muddy red water and the thorns cutting at her ankles. The story of a nation rises above her, descending from the sky to swoop down in chaotic, meteoric descent.

The woman does not look back.

Not once does she look back.

But the story of a nation catches her, as it does all other things.

PORT

Emelda Esquival ran her fingers through her daughter's hair. For the moment, Téa slept peacefully, leaning limply across her mother's chest. Emelda smiled, though she couldn't help but notice that her youngest daughter was much heavier than even a few months ago. Téa was at that age, only recently six, when children begin growing exponentially rather than incrementally. Her youngest was getting tall and lanky, too awkward and big to cradle in her mother's arms and yet, it seemed to Emelda, far too young to leave them.

Sunlight poured in from the cabin windows, bringing with

it the clean view of Rio Primero and the thick rainforest that banked it on either side.

Emelda had always heard stories about this place. Everyone in Antioch had. The first Antiochans believed the river was the source of life's beginning, that lizard men had crawled from its murky depths and onto its banks so that they might better worship the sun and sky. She'd read of the *bandas*, the vigilantes who hid in the jungle and fought off the Spanish and English alike. The jungle warlords. The river pirates.

Téa was too little for those stories, still baby-cheeked and too quick to laugh. She was a pretty thing, though, with curled copper hair and a button nose. A little red dress and a bright red bow.

The colors of her father's party.

Emelda *loathed* the idea of moving to Rio Rojo, a place she had once thought of as the "swamp capital" of the world: centered between two rivers in a region so storied, cursed, and reviled that the nation's first cartographers had named it 'the devil's cradle.' It hadn't helped when William had told her that there was an "impressive" library, one of the greatest archival collections in Antioch, patronized by the most prolific historians and writers in the nation. William thought she would be comfortable reading at home, that this was all she wanted in the world.

William didn't seem to understand that she took walks in the city alone, that Margería was a greater palace than she could ever want. He didn't know that she liked the smells of the factories, the cars, the soot and all the smoke. He never grasped that she reveled in the history of the capital, her city, which rose repeatedly from its own ashes to be one of the greatest cities on the continent.

But now, with their daughter on her lap and their three other children peering out the windows, Emelda knew that she loved her husband. That she took comfort in the safe knowledge that her husband was a good man.

He had purchased them passage on the riverboat, after all. A whole cabin to themselves.

Christopher sat in his seat with his forehead on the glass window, peering out into the jungle with a languid disinterest. He was fifteen years old, awkwardly tall and even more awkwardly voiced. The poor boy would be handsome one day, if he would only wait. For now he refused to shave his thin black mustache, or cut his thick, sprawling hair.

Edward and Victoria sat with each other, as they always did. Emelda's second son was the spitting image of his father, and at thirteen seemed as if he would easily grow into adulthood. He had his father's wide shoulders, his clean face and a low, clear voice that made him a calming presence and natural leader. Victoria, if she would ever grow up, would be stunning. Emelda saw a beauty in her daughter that she could attribute neither to herself or to William, a sharpness of her features and blue in her eyes that must have come from some distant ancestor. But for now she was still afraid of so many things, far too afraid of shadows to be anywhere near as ready for adulthood as her brother.

Emelda wasn't certain how or when the two had become so close. She supposed it was because they were only a year apart, that neither had truly known life without the other. But they always went together, always each other's best friend. At thirteen and twelve they no longer held hands, no longer slept in the same room, but they still sat together. Though they didn't speak often, they occasionally whispered conspiratorially, as if Emelda couldn't hear them.

They were scared, unsure. Just as their mother was.

Emelda stood up and paced the cabin. Téa stirred only a little, leaning her cheek into the spot just beneath Emelda's neck. The trip from Margería to Colón had been long enough, four hours of winding and bumping roads. At Colón the boat crew had been waiting for them, just as William said they would be.

The boatmen were surprisingly thin men, with bright white uniforms and smiles like cartoon wolves. They'd patiently loaded the Esquivals' belongings onto the boat. All of Emelda's books. Christopher's bicycle and his myriad of notebooks full of poems and sketches. All of their toys. Their clothes.

Then they boarded.

A thin man in a crisp uniform came through the cabin door, a white tray of sandwiches in his hands. Edward and Victoria rose from their seats quietly and cautiously. They looked from the sandwiches and back to the man.

"Hungry?" he asked.

They nodded solemnly, each taking a sandwich and receding back to their seat. The man turned to Christopher, who took a sandwich just as quietly as his brother and sister.

Emelda took one and bit into it slowly. Her stomach was empty, and this food didn't help. The meat was slick, the bread dry and the tomatoes almost sour. She had hated the idea of Rio Rojo, but now she couldn't wait to get there.

Victoria gasped and pointed frantically out the window.

If Emelda attempted to take comfort in the serenity of the jungles, of the tropical river that fed their nation, she could not deny how sinister it was when that river turned red. The color clouded the murky green, clustering in floating coagulates of crimson and brown. The riverboat continued along, turning away from the Rio Primero and into the scarlet mouth of Rio Sangria, the other river cradling the region.

The stories the tribes told about Rio Sangria were far different than those they told about Rio Primero. The Primero was the source of life, the foundational waters of the world. Sangria was a *scar*, a cut so deep that the ground could never stop bleeding. So they cursed it with legends of panthers who walked like men, of monsters who swam beneath the waters.

"It's the iron," Emelda explained.

Victoria turned to her mother, still shocked and still dubious.

"The iron and other minerals at the bottom of the river get kicked up. Makes the whole river look like blood. That's why they called it the 'bleeding river'."

"Who would want to live next to a bloody river?" Edward slipped.

Emelda couldn't see if he had any regret on his face. She had hardly hidden her fear from her children, her resentment of their situation. But out of all the people in the cabin, Edward was the one who most resembled his father.

"It doesn't have anything to do with what you *want*, Edward." Emelda found her voice colder than she meant it to be, the tone she wished she had used to answer William now being used against his son. "Who *wants* to live in a swamp? A desert? Who wants to be born and die anywhere other than where they're comfortable? It was about the same thing it always is." She looked at her son, stern-faced and tired.

"It's about *survival*. The people who made Rio Rojo *survived*. They survived the Spanish. They survived the English. They survived civil war, and they survived peace too. It was the same reason anyone stays anywhere. They would *survive*."

And they would, too.

***

William Esquival had been honest with his wife. He had spoken enthusiastically, raised his arms and pointed to the many maps that pockmarked the walls of his study. Rio Rojo *belonged* to the

Esquivals, he explained. Their family would be treated like *royalty*. William told her stories about his visit to Rio Rojo when he was a child, about the sunny, just-big-enough town with smiling people who would grin and tell him how much he resembled his great-grandfather, Thomas Holcomb.

He told her of the sprawling library, assembled by Thomas shortly after he declared Rio Rojo his "summer capital," how Antioch's first true president had acquired books from all over the world and insisted that the children of his home be no less privileged than those in the capital.

But William was not doing a good job. He could tell she didn't believe him, from the way she sighed and the way she walked away. Emelda had never been one for politics. *She* wasn't the one that needed to run away.

He hadn't told her about the letters: the ones that first arrived at his office in the Senate, and then found their way into the mail slots in his home.

In times of wealth, being a member of Antioch's Socialist Party was easy. He could wade into the crowds, descending from his stage and raise his hands high. He could clasp the shoulders of the working men, laughingly receive the kisses and blessings of their wives. Because in times of wealth, the people knew the truth. William, they knew, cared for them. He wanted the same things they did. Their children fed. Their families healthy. An opportunity for their sons and daughters. Justice.

But the times of wealth made them forget the truth: that *all* times were a struggle.

When the recession began, people began turning away. There were so many strands, so many variables beyond the simple control of any one man or woman. Their pain, their frustration, bound their vision in their short-term anxiety. Even if the party took Senate and the presidency, even if they held a two-thirds majority, it would be very unlikely that the Socialist Party could reverse course overnight. And, like any happy fool, William had told them exactly this in one of his speeches.

The crowd had booed. And the letters had started.

First came the unsigned ones, the ones that made vague promises of violence and destruction. But others came: ones that recited the senator's schedules, when he took his meals and when he left his office. Ones that knew the names of his children. Ones that detailed the various walks his wife took when he was not home. Ones signed by noms-de-guerre and drawings of bloody red swords.

William didn't want to abandon Margería any more than his wife did. He was proud of his country and its capital, at varying points better and brighter than any Paris or any London, far younger metropolis though it was. But people were being murdered. Protestors, police captains, labor leaders murdered in violent riots, or deliberately executed with a bullet.

Elías Pasqual had declared war on the country. William knew the priest from the National University, where Father Pasqual had taught a class on divinity in religion. He was a clean-cut figure in a black cassock. The priest had made William uneasy then, but now he had become something else entirely. "The Holy Swords," they called themselves. Students, only a little older than Christopher, spurred on by messianic rhetoric of a "sacred revolution."

In their letters they called William a "traitor," a "false disciple" who abandoned the revolution for political opportunity. While it was true that William had never concerned himself with the dogma of his party, he first took exception and even offense to the accusation before he understood that it was no "accusation" at all. The Holy Swords, Pasqual. They were not challenging William's legitimacy at all. Merely explaining themselves before their guns arrived on his porch.

He had secured a boat for them with the help of his colleague Senator Martin, a modest riverboat that would take them the better part of half a day to travel on. He would admit to himself, and perhaps Emelda if the conversation ever came up, that there was something peaceful about being so far removed from the world. The grey sunlight peeking through thin rain clouds. A chorus of birdsongs coming from the grey-covered forests.

Rio Rojo felt familiar, even though it had been a little over four decades since his last visit. He was only six at the time, or maybe even a little younger than his little daughter. He and his brother, Edward, had been enamored with the gardens around his grandmother's house. But now, he couldn't even remember her face. William only had a vague memory of seeing his mother carrying Edward in her arms, her face sunken and serious and Edward's wet and pale.

His mother died shortly after, leaving her young sons to a man who resented them for a wealth he would never have. Whatever happened between his mother and grandmother, it meant that neither William nor Edward would inherit anything until there were no other descendants of Thomas Holcomb left. And Edward had been dead for over decade, never meeting the son who William named after him.

In its more charming moments, Rio Rojo seemed like a quaint relic from the past. It was hardly the underpopulated village that people in Margería imagined it to be. It was a considerable town, complete with neat white-wooden buildings and well-groomed dirt roads for horse-drawn carriages. There was a large high school now, a thriving central market filled with nearly everything he could want. He had spent the day before beneath brightly colored tarps and canopies, poring over fish and meat and wondering what he would treat his children to first. The shopkeepers had smiled and waved, pointing and calling him "our senator," even though María Martin had represented the town and its inhabitants for the last two decades.

At the post office, the old woman behind the desk had dropped the package she was holding. "Señor Holcomb."

The name had been like an accusation.

William hadn't been close to his mother's family. She'd done her best to keep him away from them, telling him that her grandfather was a "good, cursed man." But Thomas Holcomb loomed over Antioch, and his sons lived wildly in the public eye. William's uncle Anthony had been a prominent senator himself, a larger-than-life figure whose love life had thoroughly scandalized his wife. When he was assassinated, the first rumor had been that it was his wife who hired the gunman. Peter was a war hero, the favorite brother of William's mother. The Holcomb family had groomed Peter for greatness and named him after a king. But he died young when his boat sank along the Caribbean coast. Then there was Uncle Gregory, the only Holcomb William could ever recall meeting other than his mother's loud, sniping sisters. Uncle Gregory, whose last words to his nephew were "You're like the devil too."

Whatever rot sat between his mother and her family had evidently spread and taken root. Now, William was the only one left to take the Holcomb name.

But when William explained this to the poor woman, that his last name was "Esquival," she merely swatted her hands and smiled.

"The name doesn't matter. The *blood* does."

For nearly a week now he had been "Señor Holcomb."

And finally, two days later, he would have to admit that he had lied to his wife.

Rio Rojo did not belong to the Esquivals after all.

***

Edward couldn't understand why his mother was mad at him. He didn't want to leave their home any more than she did. Torie came into his room the night before, crying the whole time. He hugged her and told her it would be okay even though he wasn't sure that it was true.

Christopher could have helped, but he was too moody. He used to be a good big brother, or a *present* one at least. But ever since he'd started going to high school, it was awful. He was distant, sometimes mean and intentionally cruel.

Edward regretted saying anything at all. Regretted giving his mother an opportunity to belittle him.

Silence passed between them, only broken by red water gurgling white and pink across the top. Green jungle banks, dense forests. To anyone else those jungles would have been magnificent. Paradise.

But Edward knew better. He'd heard his mother's stories. He'd read her books.

The tribesmen inside those forests had fought tooth and nail, first against the Spanish and then against the Antiochans themselves. They claimed to be the descendants of some fabled empire, the final resistance to colonization. They threw themselves against the Antiochans, against the bandas and the piratas and anyone else who would try to take their dark refuge away.

And they were not the only terror in the jungle.

Malaria. Pythons. Quicksand. Flash floods. A thousand nameless tropical diseases. Edward knew this country far better than his mother believed, and he did *not* understand how they would survive here.

Beside him, Torie was shivering. He turned away from the red water and blue skies. "Hey."

Torie had always been a pale girl. Edward believed she was the perfect mixture of their mother and father. She had their father's handsome features, his dark hair and their mother's soft chin and lithe shoulders. But she had also been tragically, constantly frightened: of the dark, of other people. Of loud noises and sudden changes. Her blue eyes, which more than any other feature were her own, always darted to corners and shadows.

Now, she was trembling furiously.

"Hey."

There was blood at the corner of her lips. But Mother was fussing over Téa's hair and Christopher's head was slouched in his hands, asleep again.

"Torie!" he hissed.

She blinked at the name only he called her. Her jaw unclenched. Her breathing fluttered as she steadied herself.

"Torie." He slid his hand to hers and patted it hard, as if he were waking her up. "Are you okay?"

"Did you see? *Did you see?*"

"Torie," he whispered. "It was only one of your terrors. You're okay here. We're here."

"But it was *here*, Eddie! It was here on the boat and in the water! It was everywhere!"

She was on the verge of tears.

"What was, Torie?"

"I…" And she stopped. She turned down to her lap. "I *don't remember*."

And his sister started weeping into her hands, cupping her mouth so that only Edward could hear her cry.

***

Christopher didn't understand why Torie was always crying.

Edward had once confided in him, complaining that Torie's nightmares were keeping her up and that, in turn, was keeping *him* up.

So tell her to go away.

He wanted to get away from his family. Father was rarely home, and the idea of following the family into politics was disgusting to him. Mother was home too much, and yet she never seemed to notice him.

Truth was, he didn't mind leaving Margería.

He wasn't handsome; Christopher knew that. He couldn't run very well or very far. His arms were thin. He could only grow a small patch of hair on his upper lip. His cheeks and forehead were covered in red-brown pimples. The girls didn't notice him, and when they did, it was only because he seemed creepy or off-putting. He didn't mean to scare anyone. It's just that sometimes he would forget that he was staring. Sometimes his mind would drift off and his eyes would stay, that was all.

But he didn't want to leave *with his family*.

He understood, though. He was old enough to read the papers. And though he had no intention of entering politics, even though the president was his godfather, and the army chief of staff was a family friend, he always followed the news with interest. General Kristoff had announced the discovery of a coup plot against the president. The offenders had been punished swiftly, he'd said, and then he stood alongside President Christopher Ambert for a photoshoot.

The army and its commander-in-chief.

Allied until the end.

But Christopher understood the end was coming, though he wasn't sure what it would look like, or if it mattered at all. He'd found the letters addressed to Father as they came through the mail slot in the door. They were signed by the Holy Swords, a guerilla group which, Christopher knew from the papers, had been carrying out raids against the military in the countryside.

The day after he found one letter, the Holy Swords took out an ad in one of the papers.

They were killing trade unionists. They were killing "fake socialist" senators. They were killing anyone who would "betray or hinder the revolution of the righteous."

Christopher sometimes hated his father, but he didn't think he deserved to die.

His mother was right; they would go anywhere they needed to so they could survive.

***

William ate his lunch at the docks.

He had not seen his wife in days, and though he supposed it was silly, he wanted to look handsome for her. He took guilty pleasure in it, catching her looking at him too long after all these years. He kept himself fit for those looks. Sure, other women might look at him that way, but from Emelda it was something else.

He took a napkin to the corner of his mouth.

The air along the river was fresh and clean, though the fishermen would bring their boats back to the docks and unload net after net of glittering silver river-fish. He had always had a fondness for seafood, but there was something to be said about the freshwater fare too. The food of a working man.

Perhaps, he mused, these were his people after all.

"Señor Holcomb."

There it was again.

The speaker was a towering man in a brown suit. Like many of the people in Rio Rojo, he seemed dressed more for Victorian

England than the jungle. He was tall, one of the tallest men William had ever met, with a thick mustache and the unmistakable ruddy tan of a farming family.

"Sorry to correct you, but my name is William *Esquival*."

The man waved. "It is I who am sorry, Senator. You see, here in Rio Rojo we love your ancestor dearly. To bear his name... it is a mark of honor. But I understand. What does a man have, after all, if not his name? If not his blood?"

The man put his hand forward.

"I am Antonio Villalobos. My family has tended to Casa Verde for three generations now."

"*You're* Antonio?"

Senator Martin had told William that the 'groundskeeper' of Casa Verde would be prepared to meet him when his family arrived. Evidently, Mr. Villalobos also attended to her residence when the senator was in the capital, and from the language of her letters, William understood María Martin to be quite fond of her attendant. Waiting in his temporary hotel room residence, William expected to be greeted by someone in dirty overalls, a stained rag tucked into their pocket. But Antonio Villalobos was a neat man, with a clearly ironed suit and a handsome, warm smile.

"Yes." Antonio's handshake was firm and friendly. "I know we corresponded only briefly, but I want you to know that I believe you are doing the right thing by coming to Rio Rojo. These people in the capital, Señor, they are like little birds in a cage. They move too fast. They think too much. They dart about and peck at each other because they believe in some ever-encroaching doom. They cannot remove themselves from their moment and see the larger swaths of history."

William had to smile. "Forgive me, it is just that you seem more...put together than I imagined a caretaker would be."

And now, Antonio smiled.

"Senator Martin does not like her staff to be informal. And besides, having access to Thomas's house means I've had access to his books. You'll find that the people along the river take the proper time to read, to educate ourselves widely."

"Is that so?"

"Oh yes." Antonio laughed and waved his hands dismissively. "I know the elites in Margería believe we are nothing but 'swamp trash,' but we won't let them forget that it was 'swamp trash' who finally united this country in the first place, will we?"

"No, no, I don't suppose we will."

Antonio sighed. Around them the sun rose ever higher; the red water gently lapped at the hulls of passing canoes and boats.

"It's been some time since a family lived in Casa Verde. It will be a pleasure to move into the groundskeeping residence with my wife. To stop shuttling between Rio Rojo and the capital."

He stopped then, turning to William with a distant sadness in his voice. "You worry about this country, don't you?"

William couldn't deny it. "Every day, it seems like there's a new riot. Every day, some foolish soldier is whisked away to prison after letting slip a loose tongue. I know our president, he's one of my best friends."

William turned to Antonio, only to find him indifferently staring into the wild blue sky.

"Yes, I worry about this country."

***

Téa was happy to be standing on the deck with Mommy. She was tired, but she was also tired of being tired. Her stomach was fluttery, and she had a dull, screechy headache. But she was tired. Too tired to cry, too tired to throw a fit.

Why did they have to leave?

Torie had explained it to her, but Téa *still* didn't understand. And the more Torie tried, the more Téa could see the little tears peeking out from the corners of her sister's eyes. Edward just told her that it was so they would "be safe," but that didn't make sense. What was wrong with staying in the capital? That's where all the soldiers were! And even still, Daddy was strong. And Daddy was important.

He wouldn't let anything happen to them.

At least wherever they were going, she wouldn't be lonely.

Mommy was turned away, looking to the sky with a limp, long cigarette between her fingers. Téa didn't like the way the smoke smelled, and wanted to go outside. To feel the warm, sticky air and listen to the "gurgle gurgle" of the river, the singing of the birds, and to smile at the bright, bright sun above them.

From the shore, the children waved at her.

They had followed her the whole way. Even in the morning she could see them. And she had never seen anyone who could *glow in the dark* before! The whole way along the river, they ran between the dark trees. They waved, did cartwheels. They danced. The most wonderful, wild, beautiful thing she had ever seen!

And from the shore, the children waved at her still.

And she waved back.

Her headache was going away.

There was a big splash!

In the red water, she could see black shadows. *Big* shadows! They moved slowly, floating just beneath the murky red water. For a moment they looked like eggs, big slow *eggs*, until they let their arms loose.

The woman's hair was glistening black. She was so pretty, just like one of Téa's princess dolls. But her skin was grey, like a concrete sidewalk. The pretty grey woman floated just along the surface of the water, waving at her just like the children. Her teeth were neat and white, her lips redder than the water.

Téa turned around. "Mommy, look!"

Mommy was tired too, Téa could tell. And she was thinking really hard, because she didn't seem to hear Téa the first time.

"Hey, Mommy!"

Mommy turned just as there was another big splash. "What'd you see, princess?"

"A mermaid! It was a mermaid!"

Mommy laughed. "No...no, probably not. But you're not the first one to make that mistake. The Spanish, when they first came to the river, they'd never seen a manatee before. They'd never seen a freshwater dolphin *either*, come to think of it."

"It wasn't a dolphin, Mommy, she had a face!"

Mommy smiled, grinning mischievously.

Uh-oh.

"You have a face, does that make you a mermaid?"

Mommy swooped around her.

"No! No!"

But it was too late. Mommy had her. She kissed her cheeks. Her neck. Téa giggled furiously.

And from the forest, the children laughed with her.

A bell started ringing.

***

Torie didn't like crying. She hated the way it woke her brothers up when she screamed. She hated the way her hands wouldn't stop shaking, hated it being so hard to breathe. Worst of all, she hated that she couldn't remember her dreams.

She knew there was something bad. Something in the river. In the forest. And it was on the boat with them.

That's what had made it so bad, that it seemed so real.

She knew she had to be strong for Edward. For everyone. She knew that they would be safer in Rio Rojo than they would be in the capital, but she was scared. She was *so scared*, and she didn't know why.

The bell rang.

Christopher suddenly jolted up and turned to the windows. Edward gasped and darted past her, moving to the row behind Christopher and pressing his face to the glass.

He called for her. "Torie!"

Again, Torie whined. Some voice in her head kept begging her to remember. She felt the ghost of cold sweat on her forehead, a soreness just behind her eyes.

But she stood up and followed her brothers.

Rio Rojo looked like something out of a storybook. So many white buildings. Towers that looked like church steeples, all lined up along a hill that seemed to lean into the sunlight. A fairytale kingdom.

It wasn't anything like what she had expected.

Despite her fears, she felt herself smile.

***

William bolted up at the sound. There would be plenty of time to talk politics, to get to know the man who had taken care of his family's home. *His* home. But when he heard the bell, William knew it was the boat bringing his family.

He had missed them, but it was only at the sound of that bell that he realized how much. It had only been a few days, but now it seemed he was physically hurting. Christopher was so sullen and so angry, but he was a good boy too. He liked to draw, to write.

The boy had a good, kind soul, and William would teach him that this was enough. Edward was so smart, so calm, so careful to act. If he wanted it, the whole world would be his.

And William's beautiful girls! God, how he had missed his princesses. His little queens. Whatever they wanted, the first thing to come out of their mouths, he would give it to them. He would turn over all of Rio Rojo just to see their smiles, glistening like the finest pearls.

Emelda.

Emelda waving from the deck!

His legs wobbled beneath him.

"Your wife is lovely," Antonio said between a soft smile.

The boat docked. William couldn't wait. He ran forward quickly.

It didn't matter. The country. The world. It was all coming apart. But they would be together, and nothing would take that from them.

***

Mundial, Issue #106

"Assassination attempt on General Kristoff foiled"

June 13, 19__, Margería

An assassination plot targeting Army Commander General Anders Kristoff was discovered by brave military officials. Led by Colonel Gardner, officers and several military cadets carried out a midnight raid against a group of senior commanders. Plotters included Brigadiers General Michael Waters, Arnolf Villalobos and Bradley Wiley.

"This is a sad day for the armed forces," Colonel Gardner told reporters. "But the enlisted should know that there are still officers who believe in them, officers still loyal to this country. Leaders such as

General Kristoff, who remain dedicated to serving their nation even in these most trying of hours."

The plotters, and those beneath them had planned to abduct the general under the cover of darkness and then kill him. As of the time of this reporting, we do not know precisely what their motives were. However, we do know that Waters has previously been investigated by military police for sympathies for the "Holy Swords," a Marxist movement under the leadership of now-excommunicated pastor, Elías Pasqual.

"To those who remain loyal to your country, I thank you." President Ambert addressed soldiers via a televised speech. "I remind you that though we may struggle now, we are foremost loyal to this nation and its democracy. I understand your pain. I feel your pain. But we must carry on, ever forward, for the glory of Antioch and its future."

The plot comes amid reports that contempt for President Ambert is rising amongst troops. Many of Antioch's enlisted come from the countryside, and it is there that embargos are hurting communities the most. Along with this, many view the president's policies towards the Holy Swords as too soft and too hopeful.

Last month, a coup plot against the president was discovered, again by young Colonel Gardner.

"Certainly," President Ambert commented to one reporter's inquiries, "we have discussed Colonel Gardner's future. And we believe that as long as our nation has dedicated servants such as him, we will survive and we will move forward."

FORTRESS

Christopher hadn't ridden in a horse-drawn carriage since he was a little boy. It was strange—though if he were to be honest, a little pleasant—to be somewhere so far from cars. Cars were too noisy, too glaring and metallic. Carriages were a callback, a reminder that there was little need to travel so fast, to go so far.

And everyone in Rio Rojo seemed to ride horses.

There were hitching posts outside restaurants. Outside the library. The whole town seemed like a mix of Victorian England and television westerns.

He supposed *he* would need to learn to ride too.

"Hey, Dad," he called up to the front of the carriage.

He hadn't stopped holding Mom's hand since they first saw each other. Christopher knew his parents didn't always get along, but it was a huge relief to see them like this.

"Hrm?" Dad called back.

"Dad, am I going to learn to ride a horse?"

Antonio laughed as he held the carriage's lines. "My boy," he called back over the clamor of hooves, "I think you'll find that everyone in Rio Rojo will be more than eager to teach a young man to ride a horse. There's an old joke here that when the women of Rio Rojo give birth, it is always to twins: first to the child, and then to its horse."

Christopher couldn't help but think of the image, and grimaced. A mewling pink baby, riding a tiny galloping pony.

"And you," Antonio continued. "You are a handsome boy. I'm sure you will find some young woman who is amused that you do not know how…and I am sure, I am sure she might teach you a great many things."

Christopher felt his cheeks burn, and reclined back in his seat. He hated that, when adults treated him like a kid. When they asked him where his girlfriend was. He hated that, because it wasn't like he didn't like girls. But they…they made him feel like he was on another planet. Like he was speaking a different language. Romance seemed easy in practice. As a concept, he *understood* it, but the idea terrified him. Made him *shake*.

As if summoned by his thoughts, one appeared.

She wore a green-and-white dress that hugged her body tightly. Her hair was dark and short, only falling to the end of her neck. On her back she carried a long rifle.

"Is it normal," Christopher heard his mother ask in a whisper, "for a young woman to carry such a thing in public?"

"Oh, sure," Antonio responded. "She is a student. Here, they are trained to shoot. I suspect this is another thing your children will be learning."

Christopher turned back, despite himself. Enough time to catch blue eyes the color of frost. A thin face and neat little nose, and a long, white smile.

She saw him look back.

She waved. Waved so high that her dress hiked above knees.

Christopher darted his head back into the carriage, mortified, curious and confused.

He turned his eyes to the carriage floor and held his hands together in his lap.

***

Emelda's voice admitted it before she could.

The sight of a young woman with such a large rifle—in public, no less—unnerved her. A black third arm stretched across her back, almost as long as she was tall.

Emelda had never once held a weapon. In her walks in Margería, she could never help but turn her eyes downward when they met the gaze of an armed soldier or policeman. She could not, for the life of her, broach the subject of her husband's past military service.

And to see someone so *young*. Only a little older than Christopher.

"Christopher and Edward both know how to shoot," William answered from beside her.

She noticed he hadn't stop smiling since they'd arrived, since he brought her in and planted a wonderful kiss across her lips and peppered her cheeks with his scratchy fuzz. In one moment all her worries had vanished, imagining his hands moving slow across the small of her back. The smell of his sweat and cologne and the taste of his neck. She noticed that he still cast her sideways glances, as her eyes were turned towards the town, and that the spot of his face just below his eyes was flushed light pink-red.

Thus, everything seemed pleasing to her husband. And while Emelda supposed that would be charming in some circumstances, to be sure in the knowledge that her husband could not help but compulsively love her, how easily he let slip that he had taught their sons to shoot prompted her to withdraw her hand from his.

Téa sat across her lap. Her little doll. Her little darling.

Her youngest was tired from the journey. Disinterested in the town of Rio Rojo, with its white rows of businesses and neatly groomed roads, Téa leaned back across her mother. With her eyes closed and her gentle breathing, Emelda recognized her daughter was close to sleep.

She didn't want Téa learning to shoot, and she didn't want her boys learning either. She certainly wouldn't give them Victoria, who was too timid to hold a gun, let alone fire one.

She would raise these objections with William later, after the man "Antonio" dropped them off at their new home.

***

Sitting next to Edward, Torie couldn't help but hold her head outside the carriage door. Everything was fascinating to her.

Like so many other girls her age, she adored horses. At the news that she would be learning to ride one herself, she couldn't help but hold in a loud squeal.

The whole village seemed like a neat little dollhouse to her. The men wore fine suits or stained work clothes, marked brown and green from cut plants and raised dirt. The two sorts walked together, waved and talked to each other and shook clean and dirty hands. And the *ladies*! They wore pretty dresses, even when they carried guns.

She didn't hear the concern in her mother's voice. Victoria, for a moment, didn't mind the thought of learning to shoot. She could be brave for them, because this place was *so pretty*!

"Eddie," she whispered.

Eddie sat in the middle of the carriage. Her brother always seemed deep in thought, thinking of some place very far away. He blinked and turned to her as if waking from a dream.

"Eddie, don't you think this place is just wonderful?"

Eddie smiled, and when he smiled she couldn't help but grin wider.

"I like it. But it's a little weird, right?"

"What do you mean?"

For the first time she saw his smile as hesitant, a half-gesture meant to put himself and everyone else who saw him at ease.

"Well," he began. When Eddie got serious, he always put his hand under his chin, something that their father did too. "Everything that *I* knew about Rio Rojo was that it was...the words Mom's books always used is 'backwards.' I expected less people. Less buildings too, I guess."

"Capital propaganda," Antonio interjected from the front.

Torie hadn't made up her mind about the man driving their carriage. He'd introduced himself as their "friend and neighbor" at the docks. He dressed nice, but his green eyes were piercing and bright. She couldn't decide if he reminded her more of a villain or a prince. He was handsome, but his booming voice and habit of inserting himself into their conversations unnerved her.

"Dear children," Antonio continued, "rest assured that nearly everything you've learned of Rio Rojo is nothing but a smear, a lie told by a few adults to make themselves feel superior to other adults. I *assure* you," he hissed, "that Rio Rojo is nothing short of a jewel of the world. And a *crowning one,* at that."

"Then why lie?" Torie asked. "If this place is so nice, why not just say so?"

Antonio leaned out over the carriage and spat. "Because it was a child of Rio Rojo who climbed out of the swamp and conquered—*united,*" Antonio corrected himself, "this entire country. Without Thomas Holcomb we would still be five warring, pathetic republics, still at the mercy of the Spanish, English, or whatever neighboring power would want to use us for slave labor."

Torie bit her lip. She had only learned a little bit about the civil wars in history class, less than she'd learned about the experience of Antioch under the Spanish and English empires. And though she knew that Thomas Holcomb was the first president of the "Unified Antiochan Republic," she also saw her teachers' eyes turn to the floor when they commented that Holcomb was "controversial."

She could see that Eddie wanted to say something, to ask another question. One hand was under his chin and the other was across his knee, fingers gently thrumming against his pants. But his eyes rested on his mother, and he stayed quiet.

***

After this, the family traveled in quiet. The carriage plodded

along past the main streets of Rio Rojo and into residential areas, enormous buildings that housed the common families of
the town. While the younger children darted about wildly, the
teenagers walked calmly and pensively outside their homes, rifles strapped carefully across their backs. Then they wound up
a long road, one that took them up a hill where they could cast
their eyes backwards towards the grand town and the massive
red river at its edge.

"Ah," Antonio called from the front of the carriage. "Welcome
home, Esquival family!"

Casa Verde was every bit as intimidating as William remembered. On his first and only visit to the house he'd felt it was awful, a cursed and cannibalistic family heirloom that swallowed
names and people whole. Its final residents were his grandmother, along with a few skeletal aunts and uncles whose pronounced
hatred for children had compelled William's mother to take her
children from the home and make them promise to never take
him back.

In his nightmares the house was looming, black and sprawling. For years he dreamed of wandering through those endless
hallways until he heard a distant, high-pitched scream. Then
he would turn around, and wake up screaming at the sight of
something he could never remember.

Even in the daylight, William was overwhelmed with the enormity of the home. However, and despite the pit in his stomach,
there was no denying that Casa Verde was beautiful. It was built
in the style of a coffee plantation, at the top of a massive hill,
with a cobblestone driveway. A long porch ran along every side
of the house, and behind it wide windows offered a view to the
inside. William counted three stories, not including the attic or
the basement, both of which he could not bring himself to visit
when he was a child.

Thomas Holcomb had built the house for himself and his wife Miranda. It was to house multiple generations, to protect the scions of an imagined royal family. William imagined Thomas had looked to medieval Europe when he'd ordered towers constructed at each of the house's four corners. The vines that climbed along the slick corners of those towers gave the house its name, crawling verdant gardens that stretched towards the shuttered windows at the top.

The land around the house was well-groomed, grass short enough to walk on. To the east of the house were stables, long abandoned, but a place where guests could house their horses. Plain wooden houses, black and rotted, where the servants used to live, were lined in neat little rows behind it.

"Are we living in a castle?" Téa asked from her mother's lap.

"It *is* a castle!" Torie answered in astonishment.

"It is, in fact," Antonio interjected once more with a jubilant proclamation, "one of the greatest, most storied homes in the world."

The family stepped out of the carriage carefully. William dismounted first to help his wife, while Antonio helped the younger children.

William watched Torie shoot off into the wide double doors. He had been worried about her, his nervous little girl. He supposed he should be glad, at ease that she would adjust so quickly to their new home. And Emelda's hand was warm in his, her body so close to his own.

"Why have we never been here before?" Emelda asked him, her eyes moving slowly along the massive house.

"We're here now," he offered meekly. He didn't want to think about his bitter uncles and aunts, or the sickly and wraith-like cousins who clung to the legacy of Thomas Holcomb as if it were the only thing they had. The only thing that could give them meaning.

William felt his hand loosen when they ascended the porch stairs.

Thomas Holcomb was inside to greet them, just as William remembered him.

His ancestor's portrait was massive, rising above two parallel staircases to the second floor. He stood proudly in his military dress uniform, red and gilded with medals, with white riding pants. Thomas's father had been a plantation owner, an English man who gave his son an English name. But he'd fathered Thomas out of wedlock, with a woman of uncertain heritage and name. The founder's uncertain parent allowed every group to claim him as their own, and the painting offered no evidence to dispute any of them.

Thomas was faced away from the artist, upwards towards the ceiling, as if in deep thought or inspiration. He had deep, brilliant green eyes and thick, curly bright copper-colored hair. A wide nose, pink lips, and narrow cheeks.

At Holcomb's feet sat Dragón, his famous dog. In the portrait, Dragón was deceptively normal, an above-average sized black lab with only yellow*ish* eyes, mostly brown. Dragón looked up at her master longingly and lovingly, pink tongue lapping at the tips of his fingers. But the dog loomed above all of Antioch, a haunting national symbol even affixed to the country's green-and-yellow flag. Though Dragón was supposed to inspire patriotism, William had experienced more than a few nightmares about the dictator's monstrous familiar. The legends and stories had been just that, folklore passed down from battlefield fog; but in them, Dragón was a looming shadow, a monster that rode alongside horses and who could bite them in two. William had grown up with these stories, with drinking songs on the lips of every soldier he had served with, about "the dictator's devil dog."

"I've seen that portrait before," Emelda whispered. "Is this the original?"

"Yes," Antonio responded from the corner of the room. "The Holcomb family took care to keep much of Thomas's original belongings. As I was telling your husband earlier, they even kept his library. His letters. They refused to turn them over to a museum, believing that one day Casa Verde might make a wonderful museum itself. And so, my family has worked for decades to keep it in pristine condition. To treat it just as we would any other sacred space."

William wanted to question him on this, the use of "any other sacred space." But he was tired, and only wanted a meal with his family. So he took Emelda's hand in his, and led her up the stairs.

***

The children at the edge of the woods were looking at her.

Téa couldn't make out their faces, because they were so small and so far away, but she knew they were looking at her. Every time she looked out the window, she saw their pale faces dart back behind tree trunks. She couldn't help but laugh at this wonderful game of hide and seek.

"This is my room!" she heard her sister shout.

She turned away from the windows. If she wasn't fast, she could be left with the worst room of all.

Torie had chosen a lovely room. The walls were brown (all the walls in this house appeared to be brown), but she had a beautiful dresser. Téa looked closer at the dresser and saw a jewelry box.

"Oooh," she whispered.

Torie turned to her sister and smiled. "Do you wanna see what's in it, Téa?"

"Yeah!"

Pearls. Golden necklaces. Shimmering rings with all the jewels she could ever imagine. Téa's mouth fell into a soft "o" before she giggled and laughed as her sister put the necklaces over her.

From the shadows beneath the trees, the children laughed with her.

***

Christopher was still sullen when they arrived. The ride up the hill made him feel more alone than ever before. His brother and sister had each other, Téa had Mother, and Mother had Father.

So he walked through the house alone, along a hallway of long windows and ornate carpets. His father was rich—a politician's salary was always a generous one in Antioch—but this wealth was absurd.

Like his father, Christopher had been largely indifferent to his legacy as a descendant of Thomas Holcomb. He'd found the portrait at the bottom of the stairs to be anti-climactic, the same one he had seen reprinted in his history textbooks. To his mind, Holcomb had united the country—merely a military leader, albeit a good one—but the presidents who came after him had done more. But Christopher thought warfare was boring and banal.

He was pleased, then, to find a wide, tall library tucked away on the second floor.

The room seemed twice as tall as the bedrooms, with shelves that went to its very top. On both sides of the wall, the shelves came equipped with a sliding ladder, something he had only seen in the archive rooms of the National Library. Christopher recognized Holcomb's desk from the portrait, and despite himself he felt a chill when his eyes went to the spot where Dragón sat in the painting. Behind the desk, two wide windows from which to survey the wide yard opened before him.

He turned from the windows and looked across the row of books, some leather and gilded and others cloth and worn. He recognized *El Cid* and *The Odyssey*. He always enjoyed the classics, and poetry. He walked slowly, touching the books and sighing.

Maybe he wouldn't be alone here, after all.

"Chris," he heard from the doorway. It was Edward, his eyes tired and a little scared. His brother was perfect. His skin was clean, free of acne or any shadow. Their parents' friends fawned over Edward, who always managed to smile so nicely without betraying any hint of force or discomfort. The same girls who snickered at Christopher would let their eyes linger on his little brother.

"Yeah?" Christopher answered back aloofly.

"You've been in school longer…" Edward began. "I was wondering…is any of what Mr. Antonio saying true? What do you know about this house?"

Christopher hated this. His little brother was curious, and reminded him at once of everything he liked and hated about himself. Edward was just as intelligent, if not more. But he was also kinder, more patient, and had none of the anger that held Christopher down like so many rocks around his neck. Edward was a better, less lonely version of himself. And because of this, all the love he had for his little brother was tinged with an irremovable bitterness.

"Obviously, it's Holcomb's old home. He built it for his second wife and stayed here during the summers. His kids built on to it too."

"Is that all?" Edward asked, meekly.

Christopher huffed.

"I don't know, Ed." He motioned to the bookcases around him. "Maybe you could learn something on your own."

And with that he stormed off, leaving his brother behind and wanting to be alone again.

***

Edward had read *Dracula* when he was eight years old. For days after, he'd had nightmares, but had been too afraid to confide in anyone, knowing how his sister suffered so much more. A tall man would visit his room, with a wide mustache and a smile full of sharp teeth, and in those dreams he couldn't escape this looming shadow as it lowered closer and closer to his neck.

Antonio Villalobos had no fangs, but looked just as much like the count as the shadow from his nightmares.

His sisters were playing with jewelry, his older brother was distant, and his mother and father were finally happy after being away from each other for so long. Edward felt impossibly lonely, and in that loneliness rose a quiet panic.

Ever since arriving in Rio Rojo, it had been welling up inside: when he saw Antonio, and the girl with the rifle. The contempt in Antonio's voice when he spoke about the capital. Edward didn't understand why his family was so welcome here. He knew Thomas Holcomb was their ancestor, and that somehow the house was in his father's name. But he didn't understand why Antonio was so friendly when he clearly hated the capital and everyone in it.

And then, Father had always said that the people of Rio Rojo were "conservative." Edward didn't know the specifics, but Father was a *socialist*. If anyone else was worried, they weren't showing it, and this only made Edward all the more concerned.

The library felt haunted. Edward couldn't help but think that these were all books that Holcomb had touched. That he had read.

And his desk. How many death sentences were written on that desk?

Whenever he asked Father about their ancestor, he grew silent. Edward had the impression that his father was uncomfortable with the legacy, as William would only answer, "A man can be both good and bad."

Holcomb had modernized the nation, Father said. He put in the canal systems, the ports, the system of riverboats that connected the country to this day. He opened schools in rural areas, made school mandatory for children, and reformed land laws so that peasants could own land. But he was a conqueror, and no amount of good could wash away so much spilt blood.

"This is my favorite room in the house too."

Edward swallowed a scream.

Antonio stood at the door, his wide smile just like the devil's.

"You are a reader." Antonio smiled. "I can tell. Quiet young men are always readers."

Antonio walked over to the closest shelf and pulled down a book. He flipped through it until he landed on a certain page, his eyes going wide and bright. He handed the open book to Edward, whose stomach fell.

It was a black and white illustration. A monstrous thing, more storm cloud than dog, running through the wreckage of a dismembered horse.

"Your great-great-grandfather was a..." Antonio paused and looked up to the ceiling, as if searching for the correct word, before he clapped his hands theatrically. "A *great* man. Capable of...so many good things. I have no doubt one of you will be as well."

"One of you?" Edward asked, fright sliding through his words.

Antonio merely smiled. There was something in his eyes, a cruel and secret knowledge, a secret he enjoyed keeping.

"You may not have his name, boy, but you have his eyes." Mr. Villalobos bent down and smiled. "This house is your seat of power, child. Use it as you will."

And just as silently as he came, Antonio left.

Edward placed the book back, unable to look at Dragón without trembling, and left the library without a destination in mind.

***

William made every tip of her burn. Her fingers felt electric across his wet, naked back, her thighs fire as she wrapped herself around him. Emelda was one sensation, one sound as they poured into each other.

Every concern vanished with deeper breaths. Every worry evaporated with their moans.

Their time together was short, nearly pathetically so. She slouched across William, his skin now cool against hers. They gently kissed each other and laughed, sighing and running their fingers along every part of each other.

"I missed you," he said. "I *always* miss you," he added.

"Mrm," Emelda responded.

"What do you think of it here?"

And with that the moment was gone, and the spell with it. With that the red waves of Rio Sangria rode up in her memory, of the girl with the long gun across her back.

"It's beautiful. But I don't want Christopher learning to shoot."

"He knows how to shoot."

"He's not a soldier, though. I don't want him to be a *soldier.*"

"What's wrong with soldiers?" William teased her by running a hand across her cheek. "You married one."

"Soldiers *die*, William!"

And suddenly his wife couldn't keep his concerns away. How many soldiers were dying today? How many tomorrow? Would they be traitors, turned in by the military hierarchy, or would they be martyrs, robbed and killed by some plainclothes guerillas?

"But it's not just soldiers dying, Emelda." When he replied, his voice seemed empty. The truth lost importance and conviction. Reality sounded hollow and very far away. "Not only soldiers."

Emelda considered his words, her eyes turned to the wide window outside their bedroom. The wider white moon, hanging over them as a brilliant glistening pearl and an amused, or indifferent, eye.

"Why have we never been here before?" she asked again.

"We're here now," he offered once more.

As he fell asleep, Emelda moved her finger through his hair slowly. The same soft, copper hair that he gave her daughter.

***

Edward couldn't sleep.

Torie was ensnared, enchanted by Casa Verde. She needed another partner, someone who was just as excited, or more excited, than her. Téa followed her rapturously, running from room to room behind her sister. Now, for the first time that he could remember, his sisters slept in the same room. Christopher went off on his own, and as always, turned his brother away when he needed help. Mother and Father had each other to tend to, and Ed was old enough to understand at least in part what that meant.

Now he walked quietly in the halls of Casa Verde, a tiny sad ghost in a sprawling haunted house.

Thomas Holcomb looked down not just from his paintings, but from every part of the house's architecture. His great-great-grandfather (a "great" man, he remembered in Antonio Villalobos's voice) had overseen every part of construction himself, spoke with every artisan, revised their plans once and sometimes even twice to fit his vision. Holcomb had designed this house intending it to be a coffin for himself, and a cradle for his family.

Edward stopped, suddenly cold and still.

He had never read about Casa Verde's construction, or about Holcomb's intent. But he found the thought, whatever it had been, was certain. Something he *knew*. Not something he *guessed*.

He turned from the walls to a wide window.

The moon hung over him, painting the whole world blue and silver.

A pale child's face looked up at him from the woods.

He blinked away a shriek, and she was gone.

Edward was alone, with no one but a haunted house.

From his painting, Thomas Holcomb smiled.

***

Mundial, issue #107
"Holy Sword presence growing, President urges calm"

June 14, 19--: Margería

Reports are that the Holy Swords, a Marxist terror organization under the leadership of defrocked priest Elías Pasqual, are expanding their presence in the northern territories of the nation. According to a letter sent to this paper by, it seems, a commander of the guerrilla movement, the Holy Swords have plans to take towns such as Bosque Buatismal and Rio Rojo, sites of more symbolic than strategic importance.

However, General Kristoff has made clear that intelligence does not suggest that the group has "much in the way of a rural army" and that the majority of guerilla activity is concentrated in major urban areas such as Margería, Candalera, and Vitterburg.

"I again emphasize to residents: be careful. Be cautious for your neighbors; we are all vulnerable, but together we can be strong."

Protestors have called for the armed forces to take over policing in the capital, as the local police have been "compromised" by guerilla forces.

President Ambert told reporters today that he has no plans to hand over the city to army policing, and has faith that the police remain loyal to the country.

"The cowards hiding in the dark should have stepped forward to the polls last year," the president proclaimed, visibly angry. "If all you can imagine as a better future for this country are assassinations and car bombs, you should have no say in it."

PÁTHWÁYS

Early in the morning, William left for town with his eldest son and Antonio.

Christopher sat intently beside the carriage driver, watching Antonio guide the horse down the curved mountain road. William sat in the carriage behind them, head leaned back against the railing so he could watch the last streaks of pink-orange leave the sky. His mind was on the unspoken conversation with Emelda. On the danger he had yet to disclose to her.

"Soldiers die, William."

He didn't speak with her about his own military career often, though he wasn't sure if it was because he sensed she didn't want to know, or if it was because it was something he himself did not want to talk about. The war with Calgería had been a brief one between two young, untested armies whose generals had only learned about war from military textbooks and their fathers' stories. It wasn't something he was particularly proud of, and he felt no urge to turn his family into one which prided itself on producing one military aristocrat every generation.

And yet, this was a hard moment. A hard moment for Antioch, and a hard moment for all of its families. In hard times, there were worse things to be than a soldier.

His thoughts drifted back to Christopher, whose eyes now seemed alive in the early morning sun, the first ghost of a smile William had seen on his son's face since arriving in Rio Rojo. Christopher was listening intently to Antonio, who was telling him of lines and turrets.

"Driving a carriage is much different than riding on a saddle," Antonio explained. "Bad riders seem to think brutalizing the poor thing, needlessly kicking it and pulling its reins, is the only way to ride. The horse then kicks them off. Blunt brutality only receives the same in kind. On a carriage, one relies on subtlety. You pull the line, but only one direction. You must shift your weight here to guide your horse, though I believe my dear Carmen knows her way to town by now."

Christopher nodded and, when Antonio handed him the line, nodded once more.

It was a pleasure to watch his son, so concentrated and so intent. So quick to learn.

Regardless of how Emelda felt, there were lessons that there would be no protecting him from. And there were lessons that Christopher would need to protect himself.

But they could put off that conversation for another time. William didn't feel guilty, and still enjoyed breakfast with his family. Simply listening to Téa try to describe her dreams in loud, halting sentences. Nor did he feel guilty for letting himself be surprised and happy when Christopher asked if he could accompany his father into Rio Rojo. Having realized how much he missed them, he didn't find himself eager for a fight with his wife, no matter how small or necessary it might be.

"Very good," Antonio's low baritone voice boomed. "You're a natural student, Señor Christopher."

"'Señor'?"

"Yes, you're becoming a man." Antonio clapped his shoulder. "And part of being a man is accepting all the dignities that come with it. Especially when they make you feel silly. A man knows when to laugh at himself, son. Not only when to be proud, but also when to be humble. Remember that: you should never feel ashamed to ask for help, and you should always feel proud when you learn something from it."

William found himself eternally grateful to Antonio.

The carriage arrived at Rio Rojo. The town was already coming back to life. Men and women moved over dirt roads with baskets of bread beneath their arms. Smoke from the various smiths and tradesmen rose into the air and mingled with the chorus-scent of hundreds of breakfasts. As he had been in town earlier than his family, William had become familiar with the unique flavor of rice in the region, the heartiness of the red beans mixed with it and served alongside sweet, lightly-fried plantain.

Though today, there was a special reason to be in town.

"There." Antonio gestured to a wooden building, an architectural medley between Victorian teahouse and old west saloon. White walls and painted green window shutters, a swaying wooden sign reading "Café Loma" in cursive blue script.

"That's where Senator Martin will see you, Senator Esquival."

William gave his thanks to Antonio.

"I have my own errands to run in town. And, if it is all the same to you gentlemen, I would take the time to see my wife today. I would like to discuss her coming up the mountain with us, and what preparations she would like me to make for her arrival in the caretaker's residence. Even a good-natured man such as myself can only be lonely for so long."

Christopher disembarked with his father, watching Antonio's carriage meld into the crowd of so many others.

"Would you care to join me?" William asked. "You may not remember Senator Martin, but she's interesting enough."

"No thanks, I thought I would walk around town a bit."

"Well…all right. Just, it's safe enough, but be mindful of your surroundings, son, okay?"

"Okay."

And like Antonio, Christopher left him. William stopped for a moment, to think on how much his son had grown. How independent he was becoming.

***

Emelda sipped the last of her bitter coffee from the rim of a cup with, she was sure, some unquantifiable historical value.

The novelty of Casa Verde was quickly wearing off. It was true that she was an aristocrat's daughter, but she had no patience sitting still for long. Now, in the midst of "Holcomb's cup" and "Holcomb's pantry" and the entire universe of objects Thomas Holcomb had once touched, held, and eaten from, she recalled her young-girl dreams with bitterness.

She sat alone in the library, gazing at all the books along the massive shelves and finding herself frustrated that she had already read each one. As a student of history herself, it seemed to her that Thomas Holcomb was a man who worshiped the past.

The histories of empires, republics, cities, emperors, and armies. With all his taste splayed out before her, Emelda found the father of the nation unsurprising and banal, though she could never say so.

Sighing, she rose from her seat. It was true that in Margería there had been a staff to clean, to order their apartment. But Emelda had taken pleasure in speaking with them, in listening to the gossip of young women and old men who were all too eager to disclose their decades-old grudges. She took pleasure in learning from their lives, and found their own small histories far more entertaining than the 'sweeping arc of nations.'

With her children out exploring the vast gardens, Emelda became determined to find something to occupy her time.

She again pored over the shelves, moving from the books with titles to unmarked, unlabeled spines. The first was a diary, though not from Thomas. Emelda found Miranda Holcomb's prose to be laughable, someone imitating a romance novel rather than living one. The second red book she pulled from the shelves was far more interesting. In it, Holcomb laid bare not his story, but the story of Casa Verde, a construction diary full of diagrams and house plans.

There were rooms and passages she hadn't noticed on her walks, secret places where she had no doubt Holcomb had hidden money and possibly weapons. It seemed there were panels behind paintings, a room in the roof of one of the towers with some sort of unspecified significance. Leafing through the pages, Emelda felt something slide out.

A piece of paper, thicker than the pages of the book.

On the bottom corner of the drawing, she saw Thomas Holcomb's signature.

But she had never seen the woman, or the child she was holding, in any history book.

***

Christopher didn't make it far into Rio Rojo on his own. He only managed to walk a few blocks after leaving his father before he was flanked by two young men. Out of the corners of his eyes, Christopher couldn't discern many details about their faces. He imagined they were about his age, maybe a year or two older. The barrel of a long rifle bounced behind the neck of the shorter one, immediately turning Christopher's thoughts to the girl he'd seen yesterday.

"You are Senator Esquival's son, are you not?" One of the voices was low, unnaturally so for someone so young.

Christopher stopped walking to get a better look. The shorter of the two had wide shoulders, and the taller was spindly and narrow. The two looked like brothers: the same brown hair and light amber eyes.

"Yes."

The two extended their hands, and Christopher shook them both. Before, being a senator's son, let alone a socialist's son, hadn't meant anything at all. He'd gone to a private school for the sons and daughters of admirals and politicians, places where the brightest children were plucked up by ancient, storied faculty, groomed and anointed to be the country's future. Christopher had been too outwardly bitter, too inwardly scared to make anything other than an uneasy, or at the very least uninteresting, impression on his peers.

And yet here, here he was already known.

Christopher smiled as the brothers told him their names, as they welcomed him to Rio Rojo and asked him what he made of the town.

"To be honest, I haven't seen much of it."

"In that case," the shorter elder brother, Andre Pervin, replied, "we'll be happy to show you."

Andre was sixteen, Michael fifteen. Andre liked hunting, shooting and running. Michael affirmed his brother's athleticism, explaining that he was fast too, but not as quick as his brother. Michael preferred riding horses in his free time, and was part of a group that regularly hiked in the jungles around Rio Rojo.

"I know coming from Margería, Rio Rojo must not seem like an exciting place for people our age," Michael added, "but it's a weird place. After all this time, people still find new things."

"'New things'?" Christopher asked.

"Rio Rojo was the sight of major battles in the civil wars. We still find abandoned guns in the caves. Indian graveyards. Things like that."

"Aren't you afraid? I heard that the Holy Sword is in the area."

"If we find the communists," Andre interjected with venom in his voice, "we just fucking kill them."

Christopher bit his tongue, afraid to ask if this meant that Andre already *had* killed, or if he was simply saying he *would*, if given the opportunity. He had never imagined the act of killing outside of history and stories, and the cold tenor of Andre's voice made it more real than it had ever been before.

"This is the school."

Again, Christopher found himself surprised by the apparent wealth of the supposed "swamp capital of the world." The schoolhouse was a two-story building every bit as modern as any school in the capital. It was considerably smaller, though, as the building taught all grades, rather than dividing campuses by age group. A large clock above the door told him it was 9 a.m., two hours past when he would begin reporting to school once he started in the fall.

"I'd be in your class, right?" he asked the brothers.

"Yes," Michael responded with a small bit of enthusiasm. "All the students in our class are fourteen through sixteen years old. I know that you might think we're a little slower here." The boy turned his face to the ground and smiled. "I wouldn't blame you for it. But the truth is that we have some very talented teachers. Most of our coursework is advanced sciences and independent studies. Once you reach the final grade, you have to present your own work. Your own contribution to the history of the town."

"What?"

"A senior thesis," Andre explained. "Every graduate must contribute to the knowledge of Rio Rojo. You'll need to spend lots of time in the library, in the forests and archives, to show the faculty something they didn't know before."

"Wow. We don't have any requirements like that in the capital."

"That's because Margería is an arrogant city." The venom in Andre's voice never left, but instead settled darkly in every cutting, harsh consonant. "It is a city so eager to surpass its history that it rushes to forget its past entirely. Forgetting the past, it has no prior knowledge as it approaches the future."

Christopher tried to laugh uneasily. "You sound like our caretaker, Mr. Villalobos."

"For several years," Michael interjected, "Mr. Villalobos was a teacher at our school."

"A teacher? Of what?"

"Of history. Ultimately, he left to take charge of Casa Verde. But not before he taught us about the rest of our vain, gluttonous nation."

"I see." Christopher remained quiet, not eager to continue the conversation further. When they spoke like this he felt guilty, both for the misconceptions he held about this place and for being from the capital. He felt that the arrogance left at his feet was the arrogance of the whole world, and that for his false sense of pride he would never be wholly welcome in Rio Rojo.

Across the way, he noticed someone coming towards them.

The blue-eyed girl from the day before.

"Alma Sales," Andre said with the first hint of warmth in his voice. "Our class president."

"Andre, Michael." Her voice was smooth and calm. Christopher imagined she would be a wonderful singer. She was a little taller than Andre, but had to stand on her toes to kiss Michael's cheek.

"And you must be Christopher."

Before he realized he was next, her lips were on his cheek. The dry, inconsequential kiss came before he could respond, flooding his head with an uneasy, though not unwelcome, warmth.

"How do you know who I am?"

Alma Sales smiled, and Christopher remembered an illustration he had seen of some fairytale wolf lurking in the darkness of its forest.

"For all its pride, Rio Rojo is still a small town. News flows faster along the river than it does in the capital. And besides"— she shifted her shoulders, and Christopher first noticed the rifle slung across her back—"your father has been here for a week, making arrangements and noise. We would have needed to have placed our heads far in the sand to be caught unaware of you and your family."

She held up her right index finger. "Senator William Esquival, forty-four; Emelda Salinas Esquival, forty-two; children Téa, six, Victoria, twelve, Edward, thirteen; and"—her wolf's smile seemed to grow wider and more mischievous—"Christopher, fifteen."

This recitation made his stomach fall. "Did my father really talk about us that much?"

She shrugged almost playfully. "In truth, I don't know what he said, only what I know."

"Our class president is also the intelligence chair of the Youth Rifle Brigade," Michael explained.

"Mr. Villalobos told me that every student in Rio Rojo learns to shoot."

"We learn more than that," Alma Sales added. "How good is your aim, Christopher Esquival?"

Before he could answer, she had him by his wrist. Her grip was smooth but firm, as comfortable a vise as there could be. "Come, and let us see."

There was no getting away.

***

Torie walked through the gardens behind Téa.

Téa looked like a flower herself, in a pink-purple dress, darting whimsically as her attention fell on one blossom and another.

Edward watched his sisters cautiously. Torie was happy, and this was the most important thing for him. His sense of protectiveness only rose with his unease. Even though the sky was soft bright blue, even though Torie was smiling and Téa was singing, he still had the impression something was wrong in this place. That this happiness would only last a moment, and then he would be the only one there to help his little sisters.

The gardens were impressive, a collection of plants from all over the world adapted to Rio Rojo's tropical climate. The hedge maze was, evidently, his sisters' priority. If his mother shared any of his caution, she hadn't shown it this morning, when she'd immediately left her children for the library. Edward would have preferred to join her, to explore the house that Mr. Villalobos had called "his seat of power," but was unwilling to leave his little sisters alone.

"Torie, Torie!" Téa called from up ahead. "Look at it!"

Edward only caught the flash of the hummingbird's wings against the morning sun, shining emerald and vanishing quickly as it came.

"Fairy! Fairy!"

Torie didn't answer, but kept her silent enraptured and amused smile.

Téa always claimed to see fairytale creatures: goblins, fairies. And while he would have preferred his sister's vision of the world, Edward was beginning to feel jaded about it. Téa was too young to be worried like him. Much too young to be scared. She didn't pause to think there was something wrong with their lives, or question why they moved all the way from their home in Margería to a place she had never even heard of before. Edward's sisters seemed happy and at ease, and despite himself, he was simmering to the point of a sour, quiet and jealous anger over their apparent peace.

"So many fairies."

The hummingbirds swarmed above them in a flowing, shifting constellation in brilliant green.

At the end of the maze were more gardens, more brilliant blooms, a white marble fountain that Edward had somehow missed from the day before: three large dogs in the midst of a primordial battle, water coming from their mouths like fire.

Edward thought of Holcomb's legendary dog, Dragón. He had been unsatisfied with the normal-seeming yellow-eyed labrador and the man whose side she rested against. These beasts, towering and roaring, seemed better representations of the stories he had read.

Across the fountain, their eyes caught his.

"Hello!" Téa waved frantically.

Torie stopped. Her shoulders stood rigidly apart, her smile gone, knees trembling.

The child at the edge of the forest was pale, so pale she almost seemed to glow. Her hair was dark and long, falling just behind the knees of her shimmering yellow dress. Edward tried to find her eyes, something that he could try and see into, but she was so far away that it seemed there were only cavernous black spaces where eyes should be.

Téa ran forward towards the forest. "Hello!"

"Téa!" Edward called for his sister, but she was already too far ahead.

The child only seemed more wrong, more out of place, the closer she came into his view. As her soft smile came into view, something inside screamed that he should turn back. As her eyes only became darker and wider, his mind began grasping for words. Her lips were moving, though he couldn't hear anything she said over the pounding of blood in his head.

He managed to catch up to his sister, wrapping his arms around Téa, who kicked and screamed, finally biting down onto his arm. But he didn't let go. Not when blood began to trickle furiously from his sister's bite, and not when Torie called to him from behind.

Because now, close, he could see her. This eyeless girl. Her porcelain smile and doll-smooth face.

And over the pounding of his head, over Téa's screaming and Torie's cries, he heard the girl's simple declaration, spoken in a whisper that somehow carried itself all the way from the forest to the pits of his stomach.

"We'll be waiting."

Behind her, he saw them. So many white faces, peering from behind the trees.

When he finally felt the hot blood on his arm, he screamed violently.

A dying fox caught in a trap.

***

William could smell Senator Martin's coffee from across the table. It was a familiar scent that invoked memories of visits to her home and office. These last few weeks only seemed to have aged her faster, her dark gray hair noticeably brighter in the café light. Her hands had always trembled, as long as he could remember, but as they paused and sputtered now, he could make out the stains and tears of age.

"The Obelisk," they called her in the Senate, the last survivor of the Holcombist Party and an ideological paradox. A known benefactor of the armed forces, who entertained more generals and admirals in her Margería home than any other senator, she was also a patron saint of labor, and could recite the names of every prominent union leader in the country. The only reason, she'd explained to William one day, that she did not join the Socialist Party, was that she saw as it 'yet another European disease' infecting Antioch.

"*Criminal businessmen. Cutthroat pirates. 'Refugees?'*" He remembered her laughing at the word, the first moment he felt he understood all her contradictions as the product of a paranoid, though calculated nationalism. "*Europe has only given Antioch diseases, poison fruit, and vampires.*"

She had taken an early interest in him in his Senate career, and quickly taught William who to go to with what prospective legislation, which chambers were always empty and which ones 'the older dinosaurs' had their affairs in.

Rio Rojo and the greater province remained the last holdout

of the Holcombist Party, and it was at Senator Martin's invitation that William had secured passage for his family. This would be his opportunity to thank her, and to give voice to what would be to anyone else unutterable fears about the future of his nation.

She wafted his thanks away as soon as he gave them word, instead snapping her long, shaking fingers repeatedly until a young man in an unseasonably hot suit brought William a coffee. Two sugars, one cream.

"One of the many differences between you and I, William, is that I do not dilute the truth. My coffee, straight from the dirt. Dark. Bitter. But warm. It is the taste of our nation, not hidden under falsities and candied lies."

"But Senator"—he smiled, realizing how much he'd missed their games—"my sugar is from Antiochan cane. My cream of an Antiochan cow, who in turn was fed on Antiochan grass on an Antiochan farm. Surely my coffee, 'diluted' though it may be, is a greater representation of all our nation has to offer."

She laughed, quick and dry. "Always justifying your bourgeois excesses in how many people your luxuries employ. I'm glad to see you here, friend."

William was glad to see her too. "My family is alive because of you, María."

"I always liked your family, William. You and that wife of yours make such *good-looking* children."

"Will you be in Rio Rojo long, or do you intend to go back to the capital?"

"Oh…William, if only you know much that very same question has troubled this dying old woman."

A genuine sadness seemed to fall straight across his back. María had announced the idea of her dying so casually, as if it were as observable and imminent as a storm heralded by dark clouds and strong winds.

"Are you sick?"

"Not of any curable disease, no." She brought her shaking coffee to her thin lips. "But I am dying. You live long enough in this country and you recognize the signs, the smell of an impending end. No, I've resolved to accept my dying gladly. It's just a question of where and how.

"In truth, I asked you here to apologize. William, you're to go on living and I'm going to go ahead, to whatever hell, heaven, or silence awaits me. My children are all dead. Can you imagine how terrible it feels? But you came into my life right as I buried a son. You reminded me of him. More than any other reason, that's why I've sought out your friendship."

William saw a phantom of tears glistening in her eyes, and for a moment imagined her hands were shaking from some ailment other than age.

"It means a great deal that you'd humor this old woman, William. This old woman who cursed at your uncle while he was her senior senator. This old woman who disagrees with you so. And I can't tell you how happy I am to see you in my dying days, though you may sadly go on living."

"'Sadly?' Why 'sadly,' María? If you've brought me here to save my life, my family's life, why should the thought make you sad?"

María huffed. The sound of horses' hooves kicking up dust filled the air as it seeped in from the windows in soft yellow waves of light.

"That's the problem with you socialists. You don't want a *revolution*, you want a *revolutionary myth*. For a soldier, William, you're one of the most squeamish men I've ever met."

"I'm not on the battlefield anymore, María."

She huffed again. "A battlefield isn't some confined space. There's no geographical boundaries. That's a comforting story the generals tell themselves so they can sleep at night, that war and violence adhere to some imagined aristocratic order. That ten-cent pervert priest Pasqual and his communists understand this, detestable though they are."

Suddenly it was as if an invisible presence had entered the room, as if an ethereal scythe wavered not only above María's head, but above the entire country. The terror infected every atom; the electricity that animals feel as some greater predator emerges from the brush whipped itself across his back in one cool wave. "Has there been any activity since I left?"

"They killed Leite," María said with the same dismissiveness she'd used to prophesize her own death. "Hanged her in her home. The theory is that someone in the cleaning staff is a member, is a communist, because there were no signs of forced entry. The police found her husband and son too—stab wounds. Bloodiest fucking thing you'd ever seen."

"My God? Leite!? And her *child*?"

"As I've said, William, there are no imaginary lines; or if there are, then we all know how meaningless they are now. 'Combatants.' 'Noncombatants.' And it's only going to get worse."

She leaned forward, and motioned William to come close too. Her voice fluttered, soft and wavering.

"The world's become interested in our tropical paradise. The capitalists are starving us. The communists infiltrating us. And let me tell you now, nothing dooms a little nation such as ours as much as the attention of the world. Poor Antioch, so cursed with such blessed, bountiful dirt."

"Are you saying you're worried about an invasion?"

María laughed until she coughed, shivering back to her repose and once again taking her coffee to her mouth. This time, a little brown dribbled from the corner of her mouth.

"No, no. The world remembers how deeply the last white

hands to dip themselves into Antioch's waters were cut. No, they'll just watch us collapse our own house of cards and then decide what role to take in rearranging our deck. But they are interested, and it's as clear a death sentence as can be given for us."

"You make this sound hopeless."

"It will only be a moment, William. A moment for dying and slaughter, but it will pass. Just as all moments do.

"I'm 'sad' because I don't know if you really will survive what's coming next. A war on foreign soil is one thing. It's not your dirt. The enemy has a different uniform. But killing on your father's soil? That's a different thing entirely."

Outside, the world grew louder.

***

Emelda heard the screams from inside the library.

It was not a normal scream, not the sound Victoria made when she was scared, or Téa made when she was frustrated. It was a long, wailing pain, made from a child's throat. She'd heard it once before, at the site of a bus accident. A grown man, crying in an unnatural high-pitched voice at the sight of his crushed, wasted legs.

One of her children was hurt. One of her babies, wounded.

Emelda ran until the whole world became a blur. She paid no mind to the height of the porch stairs she jumped over, nor the thick dirt that squelched and dirtied her shoes. She darted through the hedge maze, not concerned with the green walls but only with the loud, piercing cries of her child. She didn't notice the thorns at her sides as she whirled through the walls, the branches that tore at her as she pushed them bitterly aside.

Past the fountain, she saw her children. Victoria was frozen, and Edward was a mess of red. He held his little sister, screaming and mouth caked with gore, fast in his arms.

"Edward!"

His eyes were on his left arm, still locked tight around his sister. Emelda wept, seeing how much blood poured furiously from the wound. She unfastened Téa from him, kicking and screaming like a caught rat, and raised her son up. She remembered what medical training she had, and ripped her dress for a compress.

Téa lunged at her, scratching at her shoulders and snarling. Emelda swept back, striking her daughter hard with an open palm that sent her falling.

She didn't register the quiet that came next. How Torie stopped roaring and even the birds in the forest quieted their songs. She only felt her palms harden and strain as they came down tightly on her son's arm. The heat of his blood soaking in.

"Muh-mom."

Edward was weeping. Tears ran down his face. Emelda wanted to cry with him, wanted to hug him tight and squeeze him so that nothing could ever reach him without cutting at her own arms.

"What happened?" Emelda asked. But her voice was distant, that of an observer rather than a mother.

"She…she hurt me."

And she turned. Téa now stood too, eyes wide and glazed over, pink tears staining her face.

Emelda realized how alone they were, in their fortress on top of a hill. But she didn't feel desperate or scared; only determined, careful. She knew where the iodine was. She knew how to treat a deep cut. She lifted her son, obliviously of the burn in her shoulders and the ache in her arms.

She would dress him. She would clean him.

She would make his world safe.

***

Torie saw the girl. Torie saw the girl and something else.

A shadow, a shadow bigger than the whole world, hiding behind the trees. A shadow with yellow eyes that scared her more than any nightmare ever could. It froze her, kept her in place while Téa tore at their brother's arms.

The shadow kept her still and quiet. As her brother bled, as her mother came and ran away. As Téa cried, confused and scared. Téa was holding her now, desperately clinging at her dress and asking impossible questions.

But all the while the shadow held Torie still.

And when it was gone, the girl left too.

"I didn't do it! I didn't do it, it wasn't me!" Her sister's voice was dry and raspy, as if she had been screaming for hours before. "It wasn't! It wasn't! I'm sorry!"

But Torie didn't know what her sister was sorry for. If she didn't do it, then what was she sorry for?

Torie reached down and ran her fingers through Téa's hair. Through her beautiful copper hair, just like a doll's. She hugged her sister tightly, and cried with her.

***

The shooting ground must have been standing for years. On the edge of the perfect circle, the trees stood just as tangled and thick as they were in any other part of the forest; but when Christopher stepped in, he only felt firm even ground, free of roots and leaves. The red dirt was the same shade as the river, which he heard nearby, coming from some unknown direction through the dark of the forest.

The diameter of the shooting ground was wide, but at varying points tree trunks stood with white pieces of paper nailed to them. Christopher squinted, trying to find the center of a bull's-eye on the paper, but found nothing he could easily see.

"Here," Alma Sales announced. She held her rifle out for him with two hands.

He took it carefully. It was heavier than the small rifle he had practiced with on family trips to the countryside. Mostly wooden, with a long metal barrel and short well sprouting from it. He sputtered though, uncertain as to what he should do next.

"Ah," Alma Sales laughed. Her face slipped into a smile, and something in him burned. "You don't know how to shoot."

"I know how to shoot."

Where had Andre gone? Michael? Were they not right behind them?

"It's okay." Her voice was gentle, and he believed her.

"The first thing to do is to let me get behind you...in war, the last thing you want to shoot is a friend." She stepped behind him, like a panther. "Then, part your feet."

He shuffled his feet along the dirt.

"Shoulder width," she corrected. "A strong stance, and straighten your back."

Her hands were on his shoulders, feeling for muscles. He flexed, and expected a laugh.

Instead, she said, "Bring the butt of the rifle to your shoulder. Line your sights, and aim for the center of the head."

And he saw them. The faces on the paper. Men and women, each carefully detailed in charcoal pencil realism.

"Who are they? On the targets?"

"Enemies," Alma Sales answered as she let him go, stepping back before issuing the command. "Release the safety."

Christopher found the switch right above the trigger. He settled his sights on the picture of a man with a round face and patchy, uneven beard.

He fired.

"Good," Alma answered from behind him. "I believe you hit your target."

He switched back the safety and turned around. There was a redness in her cheeks now, and he felt a redness in his own.

"I'll go check," he answered before handing her rifle back to her. As she slung it over her shoulder, he turned away, afraid of what he would do or say if he looked at her a second longer.

As he got closer to the shooting post, a smell arose from the dirt beneath him. Something acrid and rotting, as if someone had spilt rotten meat and eggs only minutes ago.

The picture of the man was punctured, a neat hole across his left cheek. Christopher knew it was no shot between the eyes, but also that a wound through the face was likely to kill a man no matter where it was placed.

His gaze slid down the shooting post, which was stained with dark splotches, and the dirt below, a darker red than he remembered.

***

Emelda had been a medical student before she met her husband, training to be a doctor when William was first introduced to her as a handsome retired army captain. He had not yet been elected to his first seat in Congress then, but was just beginning his campaign. She'd continued her education during their courtship, beautiful and overwhelming though it was.

But one day, she wasn't sure when, the idea of having children seemed more rewarding. The act of saving lives, the joy in it, had been overtaken by dead faces. By fits of coughing, and bleeding that wouldn't stop. It was easier than she imagined it would have been, after Edward was born, to leave medicine. There were other doctors, other people who could tend to dying.

But her children only had one mother.

Standing over her bloodied son, she regretted neither her time in school nor her decision to be a mother. She found herself calm, as if she were watching her arms move through a screen from somewhere far away. It was not her who found the iodine, but the mechanical woman who stood above her child, who placed her machine arms down on his wound and pressed.

The wound was manageable. Téa had broken the skin, but not deeply. Her mouth was small, and she'd only used her front teeth. If anything, Edward was scared, not hurt. She didn't blame him, and watching her son's trembling chest rise and fall, Emelda felt herself coming back to the efficient, mechanical woman who so carefully had tended to her son.

The day before, Edward had been far too heavy to carry. The day before, he had been too incomprehensibly intelligent for Emelda to understand. How could someone so young be so smart? So responsible and so very wise beyond his years? The day before, she'd been uneasy with her son. But now in her arms he was light, and she was made of steel.

She lifted him from the bathtub and carried him to his room.

Placed above his bed sheets, the fear seemed to leave him. He looked around and Emelda remembered that his surroundings, their surroundings, were still only a day old to them.

"Edward, why did Téa bite you?"

His eyes snapped back to his mother. They quivered, shivering as they slid away.

"Edward, if there's something you feel you need to tell me, you do."

Edward nodded. He was a boy of logic and reasoning, rarely given to fits of emotion and, in his mother's simple statement, he knew there was no better option than to tell her. "It was my fault. But...I don't think I did the wrong thing."

She kept quiet, waiting for him to continue.

"There was a girl at the edge of the woods. Téa wanted to go see her. There was something wrong with her. The girl."

"What was it?"

"It was...it was just like she was out of a ghost story."

"And you felt like you needed to protect her? Téa?"

"Téa and all of us."

Emelda smiled and gently ran her hand through his hair. He looked so much like his father, like his older brother. So much like her kind, brave boys.

"I'm going to talk with your sisters. I know you're not hurt too bad, but maybe rest just a little bit, okay?"

"Okay."

"I love you, Edward. Your sister does too. Try not to be too mad at her, leave that to me."

"I...love you too, Mom."

Emelda rose gently from his bed and walked out of his room, careful to quietly shut the door as if he were already sleeping. One of the girls was already crying from behind their bedroom door.

Emelda had every intent of being angry with Téa, of scolding her for biting her brother. She was going to explain that no matter how angry you got, it was unacceptable to hurt someone else, let alone your family.

But she saw the welt on her daughter's cheek, freshly sprouting from where her own palm had sent Téa reeling. Her palm stung at the reminder, and when her wet eyes met her daughter's, she could hardly keep herself from crying too.

Victoria and Téa were both on the big bed, and Emelda rushed to them, overcome with a desperate sadness and exhaustion.

"I'm sorry. I'm sorry," she repeated, scooping Téa up to her chest. With another arm she wrapped herself around Victoria and brought her in, too. Téa clung to her, throwing her face into her mother's shirt and wailing. Victoria made no move at all, but Emelda didn't notice.

For what seemed like hours Emelda held her daughters, their sobs slowly turning to soft sniffles and finally to tired, haggard breaths. She was tired. So tired. But she needed to talk to her daughters.

"Téa, sweetie. I'm so sorry I hurt you. You scared me. Do you understand? You bit your brother and I was scared."

"I know, Mommy. It's okay. I'm not mad."

"But Téa...*why* did you bite him? That's not a good thing to do."

"I was...I was scared too."

"Of the girl in the woods?"

Téa shook her head, but Victoria yelped.

Emelda finally noticed her eldest daughter was rigid, her muscles pulled tight and hard. She noticed Victoria was cold to the touch. She gently released Téa and turned Victoria towards her. "Victoria?"

"There's something in the woods."

Her voice was so soft that Emelda had to lean towards her, even though she was so close.

"It's everywhere."

***

As William returned home with Christopher, he found himself quiet.

Something had stirred his son, giving him a soft smile and reason to hum from behind closed lips. Part of him wanted to ask, but another, more powerful part couldn't look away from his son without imagining what would have happened had they stayed even a week longer in Margería.

Katrina Leite had been the first woman elected to the Senate from the Socialist Party. William once held campaign rallies for her, and hosted dinners in her honor. She was a brilliant woman, a true intellectual who could recite the classics of both literature and philosophy from memory. Her husband Sebastían had enjoyed fishing and hiking, and had wanted to take his boy fishing along the Rio Primero when he was old enough.

Their boy.

Alexander.

Only thirteen. Edward's age.

What sense did it make? What political agenda was furthered with the slaughter of a child who'd never engaged in politics? Who did it satisfy?

Looking at Christopher now, he could only dwell on a slaughter narrowly avoided. The evening light cast the whole world in a sanguine orange-red, and it wasn't so hard to imagine his son's face cut, battered and broken.

"Christopher," William finally said.

Whatever dreamy haze held him was broken. "Yes, Father?"

"I'm going to teach you to shoot."

"Oh. Actually, I met a girl today, she's teaching me—"

"Ah ha." From the driver's seat, Antonio laughed. "I *told* you, Señor Christopher! Perhaps I should add 'prophecy' to my many talents? Tell me, what is her name, perhaps I know of her?"

"Alma Sales," Christopher responded bashfully.

"Ah! A former student of mine. A brilliant young woman, to be sure, but also a treasure. Should you be lucky enough to become ensnared, I would advise you to not fight it. I knew a young woman once, so beautiful and terrifying I thought she could command the sky itself. She demanded first that I love her, and then that I marry her. Those happiest commands! How they've made a better man."

"Christopher," William interjected into their banter. "You may be learning how to shoot like a man, but I need you to shoot as something more.

"You need to learn how to shoot like a *soldier*."

***

It was a hard dinner for Torie.

Immediately she regretted opening her mouth to her mother, telling her about the shadow behind the trees. The girl, Mother could believe. When their father came home the first thing her mother said to him was: "There are children coming up from the town and scaring the kids."

Mother had believed Edward when he talked about how he felt something wrong. That he was scared. But when she told Mother about the darkness behind her, the thing that submerged all the light around it, Mother had only reached for her forehead and said, "Oh Torie…you're a little hot."

The quick dismissal only made Torie throw her head down onto a pillow. Her little sister, now sufficiently consoled, softly lay across her sister's back. But Torie wailed until she fell asleep, her mother's gentle singing only stinging even more because it was full of pity.

At dinner, their parents fought.

Mother had cooked something quickly, rice and beans with grilled chicken that tickled with black pepper. It had been nice although quiet, a calm, unarticulated sadness that had been manageable until Father had said he wanted them to learn to shoot. Not just Christopher and Edward, but Torie too.

Torie thought of the shadow. She didn't think a gun would do much against it, but she would be willing to try.

Before Torie could even say she was interested, Emelda stood up. There was an anger in her eyes that Torie had never seen before, not when she'd slapped Téa off of Edward or when their parents used to fight in the capital.

"No," she said coldly.

"They need to learn to defend themselves," was Father's response. "You don't know what's coming, Emelda!"

"And what is that, William? What has you so scared that you want to give our children guns?"

"Katrina Leite is dead! They killed the whole *family*, Emelda!"

The proclamation sat heavy on the table.

Torie remembered Alexander. She'd thought he was cute, but he was also funny. When other boys were so mean to the girls they liked, Alexander always just made them laugh. He could juggle, and he could balance pencils on his nose. He spoke fluent French, and one day he'd left a piece of paper with poetry written on it on Torie's desk. When he translated it, she felt with such childlike certainty that this was the boy she would love forever. Compelled by this realization, she'd firmly announced that she was going to kiss him. He seemed just as surprised as she was, just as afraid when she closed her eyes and leaned into his lips. And when it was her turn, she trembled too. Somehow that had made it better, that they were both scared together.

She'd never told anyone about that. But she did leave a note at his house before they went, telling Alex where they were going and that she hoped he would write her. She wrote she was sorry, but her family was scared and she wanted to be with them. That she was sad, but maybe "goodbye" wouldn't be forever.

And when she wrote her 'I love you,' her heart had fluttered furiously.

She'd never know if he read her letter. If he felt just the same. Or if he was too scared to remember her when he died.

Dead.

Torie ran from the room, uninterested in whatever fighting her parents needed to finish. Already exhausted from crying, she could barely keep her eyes open.

As she closed them, she hoped she would dream of Alex, so they could be scared together.

***

Mundial #108
"State Funeral for Katrina Leite"

June 15, 19_____, Margería

For a moment, it seemed that Margería was a sea of red as support-ers of the Socialist Party came to show their support and sorrow. Katrina Leite (42) found dead in her apartment with her husband Sebastián Olán (44) and son Alexander (13).

Born the daughter of two farmers, Senator Leite had enormous hurdles in her early life. Her eldest brother, Peter, was killed by yel-low fever when she was 12. The next year, the same disease took her younger sister, Anna.

Leite was the only surviving child of her parents' marriage, and made an effort to carry her family name far. Receiving first the Ed-munds Scholarship and then the Frankel Award, Leite was able to attend the University of Antioch in Margería for her undergraduate and graduate studies. There she became involved in several student activist movements, protested austerity measures by the Kleine ad-ministration, and first met her husband. At 36 years old, Leite was the youngest senator elected in Antioch's history.

Several speakers delivered their own eulogies.

President Ambert said of Leite, "I have never met a more exceptional fighter in my entire life. Those who knew Katrina would describe her as unyielding. I always knew when we disagreed that I needed to re-examine my position, because Katrina would not dig in unless she believed hers was a cause worth fighting for."

Notably absent was fellow Socialist Senator William Esquival, whose friendship with Leite is known. A spokesperson for Senator Esquival's office could not be reached, fueling rumors that the senator has fled the capital.

Posthumously, Leite has been awarded the Medal of Valor, the highest civilian honor available, by President Ambert. She will be buried with her family, but authorities are taking care to guard the location of her final resting place.

Though the Holy Sword has been implicated in the killing, others are skeptical.

"She was a woman in politics," one source said. "The ugly truth is that the very fact she existed was a personal challenge to so many people. She had no shortage of enemies, as sad as that is."

At this time, no arrests have been made. The military police declined to comment for this piece.

ARMAMENTS

William spent the night away from Emelda, and as in the week before, it seemed an almost physical pain that rested just beneath his chest when he was away. His sleep had been uneasy without her, burdened by María Martin's warnings and his imaginings of the last dying moments of Katrina Leite. As he almost fell asleep, a far too gruesome thought entered his mind.

Had they killed Alexander before they killed her?

With that he abandoned sleep, walked from the spare guest-room and down into the basement.

The rooms beneath the earth were humid, and lined with thick stone. In the light of his dim yellow lantern, the basement seemed to expand forever in all directions, and this endless quiet loneliness seemed far more comforting to William than the goings on of the world above.

He found the metallic green trunks exactly where he'd left them, in a far corner where he hoped neither Emelda nor their children would find them. Unlatching the trunks, he realized how long it had been since he held anything from his military career.

The war with Calgría had been a short conflict, fought between two young brother nations with little experience at war. Fought by the grandchildren of the wars of rebellion and unification, the war with Calgría was the product of generals and politicians in both countries who wanted to stake their claim and make a point.

"A point." Over a disputed forest. A place too densely wooded for it to be of any immediate use to either Antioch or Calgría. In the end, both governments agreed to a truce, using puffed-up language so that an undignified draw could be dressed up as a victory.

William only knew one politician who supported the war, only one who didn't regret their vote and propaganda that had sent over twelve hundred troops to their death.

María Martin, who'd told him in the face of his accusation that the war only proved Antioch had a willingness to sacrifice its boys for a spot of useless dirt that, "Sometimes it is useful for a nation to remind her neighbors that she will be willing to die over trifles. It's a warning to not trifle with her at all."

"Only to die over dirt?" he had replied, angry that this woman who had never been to war herself would so dismiss the notion that some things were categorically not worth dying for.

"The highest calling of the patriot," she had answered with such steely certainty, *"is a man's readiness to die for their dirt."*

Opening the trunks, he found his old rifle, by now an outdated antique compared to the modern equipment of the army, and then his standard-issue pistol. He remembered at first how heavy the rifle had been in his arms, when he was a young man of only sixteen. But since then he had held so many other things in his arms—his children, his wife—and now the rifle felt light, inconsequential. In war, it had been the thing he could never lose.

The pistol seemed so much smaller, now that he had held his daughters' hands. It was light, with a long barrel and thick handle. Téa would have no problem holding it if she held it with two hands. Edward, either.

He took the guns up the stairs and out into the garden.

In the hours before dawn, the sky was still black and the moon hung high and bright enough to cast the whole world in grey light. The stars seemed cool, like ice water running over the roof of the world. The woods at the perimeter of their land burst with sounds, millions of insects and night birds blasting their chorus that somehow only amplified the quiet of this world.

He enjoyed the stillness for a moment, only a moment, before setting to work.

As the sun rose, he found where he would place the targets his children would shoot.

***

Emelda heard her husband moving through the house and tried to bite back her tears.

The Leites were not strangers to her. To a certain extent, she'd considered Katrina a friend. True, they had never met outside of the company of their husbands, but they had always found each other at parties. It was a silly thing, but Emelda enjoyed someone who could talk about both being a mother and being something other than a mother. She loved her family, but too often those who talked with her only wanted to tell her about their children, their husbands, while never once mentioning a thing about themselves.

In contrast, Katrina could talk about both. She was a friend who took an interest in Emelda's thoughts on politics, on literature and the modern sciences. She was someone who could then turn and sigh, mentioning how she'd caught her son drafting love letters to Victoria.

Victoria.

She had been so hurt by William's news, of both these unwelcome deaths and his intention to arm the children, that she hadn't thought about her daughter's own hurt. Emelda's own first love had been a much older boy, a fifteen-year-old who'd sold bread at his mother's bakery. Emelda's mother had caught on to her innocent infatuation and made daily stops with her young daughter to the bakery.

But it was, of course, unrequited love.

Victoria and Alexander never told their mothers about their sweet little love, but children are only so good at hiding things.

The thought, though, of a gun in her children's hands upset her deeply. It was true that William had come back from Calgría, but Emelda's older brother never did. Carlos had been eighteen when he was drafted, an easy, carefree young man who wanted to marry the girl at the flower shop. When he came home in a pine box, the girl threw herself over the crate as if it were the only thing tethering her to the ground.

Carlos had been their father's favorite, though Emelda was never jealous of it. She considered it natural that Adolfo Salinas would gravitate towards a son who so looked like him, who shared his interests. And Carlos had a warmth around him, a warmth possessed by very few people, a sort of power to set others at ease or capture their attention at will. It was a warmth she had desperately missed until she met William.

But Adolfo Salinas died shortly after watching his son's fiancée throw herself over his coffin, leaving his daughter to be a sad, though wealthy, orphan at the age of sixteen. Adolfo's quick descent into alcoholism had more than motivated Emelda to pursue a medical career.

She didn't begrudge soldiers, didn't begrudge war. To her, it was only a question of grim odds. Who would come back and who would not. A person could be smart, a person could be cunning. A person could even be kind. But all were subject to an iron law of probability. To hold a gun was to increase the odds that you very well might die by one.

Emelda couldn't stand these thoughts. This insomnia, the sound of William digging for the weapons that could doom her children.

She threw her bed covers off and slipped into a nightgown. Now, while nearly everyone was asleep, she could set about searching the house for the secret rooms she had found on the library's map. She had placed the map by her bedside, planning to excitedly announce her discovery to William before they fell asleep. It was to be their own private adventure, a small thing that they could do together without leaving the house. But now it was diversion, *desperate* diversion to pretend she was anywhere else.

At night, Casa Verde seemed like a gothic palace. True, there were no stone walls, no torch-lit hallways, but the hallways were wide and cavernous nonetheless, the wide mouths of deep-sea monsters rising to the surface. The lantern in her hand didn't allow her to see far, only a few steps in front of her. She thought of Theseus and his labyrinth, of Hansel and Gretel and their trail of bread crumbs. At these thoughts, she couldn't help but laugh at herself, a grown woman scared and unnerved in her own home.

The apartment in Margería had been well curated and decorated by Emelda herself, who treated the home as if it were its own organism. A home's health, in her unspoken theory, would reflect back on the health of those who lived within it. So she'd selected the artwork, the flowers, the furniture and carpets. In truth, she had not been the master of her own space until she lived with William, who had a typical, banal male disinterest in decoration. Growing up quickly in her parents' home, she never found a moment to arrange a place for herself. Then it was one dorm after another, where spaces and living were so strictly choreographed by faceless deans and alumni that she sometimes imagined she knew how her husband must have felt in his barracks.

At night, Casa Verde was hardly her home. Another painting of the house's father and master; she had no doubt who the house belonged to, and it was not her.

She moved up a flight of stairs, farther away from William and her children's bedrooms on the second floor. The third floor seemed useless, considering how small her family was. She wondered if Holcomb had wanted it less for functionality and more for a symbol of status. She could not, however, deny that it held some of the best views in the house. From a wide window she could see the gardens, the forest, and the deep, red running scar of Rio Sangria as it lashed and coiled along the side of the town.

Beneath the stars the town of Rio Rojo seemed medieval: neat

buildings and towers that would deceive those who didn't both-
er looking beneath the city's surface. "The swamp capital of the
world," she remembered she'd once called it.

Alone above the city, she decided she would leave the house in
the morning. If William wanted to put a pistol in their daughters' hands, Emelda would not allow herself to witness it. She
would go into Rio Rojo and she would see it for herself. If the
town had nearly as many secrets as Casa Verde, she would need
to know them. She would talk to that fascist witch, María Martin. She was a detestable woman, but knowledgeable of all things
related to Thomas Holcomb.

The map indicated that she should turn into a bedroom.

The room was still furnished fully, ornate wooden beds with
curved posts and a writing desk with a bottle of wet ink on the
table. She moved to the table and lifted up the bottle, finding
there was no dust on it at all.

Antonio had told them it had been a long time since anyone
lived in Casa Verde. He was the groundskeeper, but was he the
only one? How could one man take care of all this home.

She set the bottle down and surveyed the map again. There
was a room behind a large wardrobe. The thing was impressive, dark oak wood that strained the entirety of her back as
she pushed it towards the corner of the room. She hoped her
children were sleeping deeply, that Torie had cried herself into
a numb sleep, and that the others were too tired from a long,
difficult day. The wardrobe gave way only slowly, grating against
the wooden floor with a screech. Emelda huffed, pushing it until she felt it make contact with the corner walls.

She saw a layer of glittering dust on the secret door, one in-
dicator that there were parts of Casa Verde that had not been
rigorously and religiously maintained by its unknown cleaning
staff.

There was no doorknob, but a circular hole where one should be. She put her fingers through to the other side. It was cold, so much colder than the room around it.

The door swung open, and Emelda stepped into a mausoleum.

The room was neat, but covered in dust. She brought the sleeve of her nightgown up to cover her mouth as she peered around. There were three paintings, one on each wall. She recognized the woman from Holcomb's secret drawing, though now she was rendered in full color. Short blond hair the color of sunflowers, green eyes that shimmered out like the forest in daylight. In the first painting, she was holding the hand of a young man who sat next to her.

Emelda squinted, motivated by some absurd instinct that told her if she examined the man's face differently, it would somehow change. But unmistakably, the man she saw was a young Thomas Holcomb. There was no mistaking that deep auburn hair, or his indistinct tan that had led historians to postulate that the founder of the nation could belong to any given ethnic group. He held this woman's hand and smiled at her with a familiar look. Whoever the artist was, Emelda couldn't help but marvel at their ability to render love so effectively.

In the second, she was walking in a forest path. She wore a white dress and a blue ribbon in her hair. She looked back over her shoulder, as if calling back to someone. Turned slightly, Emelda spotted a slight bulge beneath her white dress.

The third was directly opposite of the door. The woman held a child. A little swaddled thing with a fat face. Thomas Holcomb stood behind, his hand on the woman's shoulder.

Emelda walked forward, looking at the gilded nameplate at the bottom of the painting's frame.

Elizabeth Holcomb: with husband and child.

***

Edward had not even climbed into bed when he heard a knock at his door.

Opening it quietly, he found Téa, her lips trembling and eyes quivering. How much of her day had been spent crying? He knew he should be angry with her—his arm still hurt, and he had a dull headache from the stress—but seeing her dry red face, he only wanted to hug her.

"Eddie," she began. "Can I sleep with you?"

"What's wrong, Téa?"

"Torie is crying...she hasn't stopped crying since dinner and I don't wanna cry anymore." She looked at him meekly. "You won't cry, will you?"

"No, come in. I won't cry."

She was so small under his arm. She climbed into his bed and he followed her, giving her room and taking only one pillow for himself.

"Eddie?" she asked.

"Yes?"

"Are you mad at me?"

Edward paused, trying to think about what he felt. Téa was a temperamental child, quick to anger and capable of throwing a fit when things didn't go her way, but she'd never hurt anyone. When she'd learned meat came from animals, she'd spent the whole evening weeping, and Edward had to tell her that the animals didn't hurt, that they knew their whole purpose was to be meat. The lie was essential in calming her, because Téa couldn't stand the idea of hurting something.

"No, I'm not mad at you, Téa. You're a good little sister. A bit of a brat, but you're a good little sister."

"You're a good big brother," she said.

"Thanks."

"But Eddie…I don't know why I did it."

He didn't say anything to that. He let her be quiet for a moment. "Who was the girl in the woods, Téa?"

"I don't know. But they want me to come play with them."

"'They?'"

"There's so many of them, Eddie. So many kids who live in the woods. They showed me. They showed me all the way up the river."

He didn't understand what she was saying, but a lash like cold water went down his back. The night seemed darker now, the window too full of dark, evil potential. He leapt up, moving to draw the curtain, when he saw her.

Glowing from beneath the cover of tree branches.

He shut the curtains furiously and ran back to his bed.

"Téa," he whispered. His teeth were locked, biting down on each other until they hurt.

"What's out there, Eddie?"

"We have to stay away from them. Promise me, Téa."

"Eddie—"

"Promise me!"

"Okay…I promise."

He pulled her close. "Thank you, Téa."

Long after his sister fell asleep, he could feel eyes on him.

In the woods below, the children gathered, smiling in the night.

***

In Torie's dream, the water was red. There was no darkness in the crimson except for the bodies, which floated and swam like so many drifting black stars.

In the red water she could see them clearly, so many specks of life dragging, spinning like angels in the sky.

They passed her by with wild smiles, with black eyes and gleaming shark teeth.

Some were naked, bloated pale things that shined like the underbellies of wet lizards. Others wore neat clothes, tailored suits and fine dresses that clung to them like moss clinging to a branch in a running stream.

In this constellation of faces and limbs, Torie was frozen. A scream was dying just behind her throat, which could only produce dry, grating cough-like sounds.

She wanted to swim to the top, to look for anything resembling the sky. But in all directions it was only red. Red water and drifting bodies.

Slowly a small form, only a little bigger than herself, floated towards her.

No.

She recognized the black school uniform and the back of the boy's neck, the hair that rounded it.

No.

But she couldn't say anything at all as Alex's face turned towards her, pale and eyeless. From his mouth, a trickle of blood floated up.

She awoke drenched in sweat and gasping for air. Her whole body hurt as she breathed in and out, immediately assailed by the recent memories of the hard day before. She didn't scream. She wouldn't scream.

Everyone else was scared too, and she needed to be strong. She would learn to shoot. She would learn to be strong.

The window was open, drafting a cool humid air in. She rubbed her eyes, still stinging and raw from tears.

At the edge of the woods, the girl smiled at her.

And behind her, the shadow again. But now it had eyes. Two brilliant yellow things that glowed even brighter than the pale girl's skin.

"I hate you," Torie whispered.

She closed the curtains, and imagined how a pistol would feel in her hands.

***

Mundial #109

"Reports of the Holy Sword in the Devil's Cradle"

June 15, 19___:

Several sources have reported that the communist insurgency has taken root in one of Antioch's most storied regions. Between the Rio Primero and Sangría, the Valle Norte (popularly referred to as 'the devil's cradle') is a fertile marshland known for its dense jungles. Rio Rojo is the only major urban area in the region, and is considerably isolated from the rest of the country.

Should the communists be able to infiltrate the surrounding area, observers warn that the town could be isolated. The same observers also said, however, that Rio Rojo serves more economic and historical importance than strategic significance.

As the birthplace of Thomas Holcomb, guerilla propaganda would postulate that the Ambert administration is incapable of defending a place of historical national importance.

The province's senator, María Martin, dismissed concerns about the insurgency taking the city:

"As I have tried to make clear in my long career representing Rio Rojo, our people are far prouder and stronger than the vast majority of their countrymen. Should the communists wish to try, they will find me with my people. Armed and ready."

Since this proclamation, we have spoken to Senator Martin's staff, who have confirmed she has returned to her birthplace.

ENTRENCHMENTS

Emelda could not find it in her heart to talk to her son, not this morning.

When she announced her intention to go into town, Christopher said he would come along too, but too eagerly.

"Why?"

"There's someone I want to meet."

Only a day here and he had found someone, maybe his *first* someone. Only a day later, her son was a far cry from the sullen, angry boy he had been before arriving. His eyes seemed to shine a little brighter, his smile more natural and easier-going. She could see the outline of the man he would become easier now, and witnessing it her stomach fluttered.

Some playful, motherly animal in her wanted to tease him, to reach for his cheeks as she had done when she was a child and sing, "There's my favooooorite smile." But then, it was heart-breaking that he was growing up so fast.

Fortunately for her, Antonio had apparently taken to teasing him. "Are we looking for young Miss Sales today, Señor Christopher?"

"Yes." Christopher answered straightforwardly, even eagerly.

Why was it that boys were so eager to talk with anyone else about love, infatuation, than with their own mothers? Why was Antonio's teasing almost welcome, whereas hers would only be met with anger? But then she thought of William, and the steel anger in her soul welled itself up to the surface of her thoughts.

How dare he?

"Then if I may offer some advice," Antonio seemed to venture from his coachman's perch.

"Yes?"

"Yesterday I joked of a commanding woman, but I must tell you that sometimes men enjoy teasing women even when they are not with them. A man is most at ease when he is most himself. And he knows he is most loved when someone loves him so. Do you understand?"

"I…no?"

Antonio laughed. "I am saying that if you are yourself, you will be far better off than pretending to be someone else. Have some faith in yourself, Señor, and it will show."

Emelda could have kissed Antonio then.

The ride down to Rio Rojo was much shorter than the ride she had taken with her family when they'd first arrived, what now seemed like years ago despite only being two days. Already she felt something was different in the town's air, that there was something heavy and unspoken beneath the smiling eyes of the people out in the street, who waved to each other as they quickly moved forward in their day.

"And here we are, Señora Esquival."

The café beneath the hotel where María Martin was staying was already full of customers, wafting out the sounds of gossip, speculation with the scents of strong coffee and buttery sweet breads.

"Thank you, Antonio."

"It is my pleasure, Señora. And please, give the senator my regards. While it is my pleasure to service the family of Casa Verde, I do miss my kind employer."

Emelda stepped off the carriage, catching bits of how Antonio was willing to take Christopher a little further into town, knowing a spot where 'Miss Alma Sales' could be frequently found with other students during the summer.

The café doors swung open and she scanned the crowd. Mostly men, independent and reading their newspapers away from home as uniformed staff brought them cup after cup of light-brown coffee.

María Martin sat in the corner.

She looked more youthful than Emelda remembered, though she would be the first to admit that she went to pains to avoid contact with the senator. Unlike Katrina Leite, Emelda found nothing worthwhile in María Martin. To be sure, the woman was friendly enough outwardly, but her warmth always recalled that of a fairy tale witch, extending her clawed hand with a poisoned apple before latching on to your wrist and taking your whole arm.

For someone with his background, so intimate with human cruelty first at the hands of his father and then those of war, Emelda found her husband bewilderingly naïve when it came to his own profession. To keep a friend like María Martin, whose toxicity was apparent to anyone who spoke with her for more than ten minutes. Honestly, Emelda was surprised it had never cost him an election.

María Martin looked up at her, first in surprise. Did Emelda spot panic there? A quick shaking of her irises? A snarling, lupine growl? No, because the moment Emelda stepped closer, those eyes were warm and open like a murky green tropical bay. Her teeth were as white and clean as ever, as if the old woman hadn't consumed a lifetime of coffee.

"Emelda!" Her voice was excited, almost grandmotherly. María stood quickly and rushed, leaning up to throw her withered arms around her neck and plant a dry kiss on Emelda's cheek.

"Senator Martin." Emelda only had it in her to act under the pretense of kindness for so long. Telling William about Katrina Leite had been one thing, but she wouldn't forgive this woman if she had told her husband to arm their children. And besides, María Martin was the last sitting member of the Holcombist Party, and a known biographer of the former dictator. Antonio was responsible for taking care of the house, but María Martin paid to keep it like a private, personal museum before Emelda and her family came to Rio Rojo. María Martin would tell her, among many other things, who had keys to the home where her children slept.

So Emelda returned the senator's kisses, her bitter-honeyed false smile that seemed to split her wrinkled face. She joined María Martin at her table, and took her coffee black as the senator's.

"It is my immense pleasure to receive you and your husband both in the same week, I cannot tell you how I treasure his company and the sight of you."

"You're too kind, Senator." Emelda sometimes found joy in small talk. There was a sense of relief in talking about nothing, in hearing her own voice and that of another. But with someone she wanted something from, it was only more politics. With María Martin, it would grow old fast.

"How was your trip up from the river?"

Emelda answered that it was long, uncertain. She had known so little of Rio Rojo, only its notorious reputation in national myth. At the words "national myth," the senator let loose a small smile. Emelda then described Casa Verde, how beautiful the walls of ivy vines were, the sense of history in its walls, peppering her recounting with lies. Lies that being in Rio Rojo and Casa Verde had inspired some new sense of pride in her, a pride in her nation that was different from what she'd felt in all her years living in Margería.

"They call this region 'the devil's cradle,' which is fine. To be honest, my dear, I rather like the name. But what it really is, is the cradle of the whole nation. Every rebellion, every rebirth began here. In these marshes. On these hills, nestled between our two rivers, every bit as grand as the Tigris and Euphrates."

"You've written a few histories of the region, Senator. I was actually wondering if I could ask you about that."

"Heh. My dear, every politician is flattered and eager to discuss their areas of expertise, you need only ask."

"Thomas Holcomb. In your biographies you say he married once, to a woman named Miranda Castellanos."

"Correct. The daughter of a local sugar plantation-owning family here in Rio Rojo. Miranda, you know"—the senator leaned back against her bench as if pleased with herself—"actually fought in the unification herself. Should I not die before the end of this year, I have compiled enough material for a book on the history of women in the war of unification."

"Then do you know if Holcomb had married before?"

"A secret marriage?" There was a genuine concern in María's voice; the mere possibility of her hero having some moral blemish, some hidden affair, seemed to frighten her.

"Perhaps not 'secret' so much as 'forgotten'," Emelda offered. "To a woman named Elizabeth?"

The senator's mouth formed a small 'o.' She huffed, a sigh of relief that went up with a shaking wave of her hand.

"In some of Holcomb's diaries—which I have reviewed, though I have not reviewed them all—the Founder was a prolific writer. In some entries, he alludes to one 'Elizabeth.' Elizabeth Salazar."

"What does he say about her?" Emelda felt her anger and venom subside, overtaken by some ominous curiosity.

"He describes her sadly. He misses her."

"Anything else?"

"No. Whoever, whatever she was to the Founder, I always got the impression that she died young. Of natural causes. In those days, typhoid fever was a true killer in the devil's cradle. It's a miracle that the Founder lived through it himself, being born as small and frail as he was.

"I'd imagine it was a romantic enough story, but how romantic is a young boy's love, still untested by hardship? No, no, I think the far more romantic story is of the woman who rode by his side into battle, who commanded her own troops and spilt her own blood. That's the more important story for our nation. The more interesting story, I'd think you'd agree."

"So then, what, Elizabeth's story goes uninvestigated? Unreported?"

"I had no interest in it, Emelda. A person's life is full of so many insignificant loves. And no matter what they may think, most loves are so banal and uninteresting to the great eyes of history. Like any meaningful ore, history needs to be made use of before it has any real value."

"So you've excluded her from your books because you found her uninteresting? But you have a whole chapter on the genealogy of Holcomb's dog."

At that María Martin laughed. "Again, Emelda, you may think it cruel to say: but a first love is like a first shit. We've all had them, but they very rarely mean much."

Emelda offered her own bemused smile. "You don't have much of a sense for romance, do you, Senator?"

Around them, the café began to crowd, men and women coming in to meet over plates of eggs and the thick scent of coffee.

"Not anymore, no…Emelda. But if you can believe it, I loved my husband. He wasn't my first love, but he was the one who mattered most. We had children together, and by the time he and I had grey in our hair, we had already buried one of them. Now he's gone, and so are the other two. So no, now I'm afraid all my romance is gone."

Emelda didn't allow herself to think on María Martin's story for too long, lest she come to feel sympathy for the woman. Talking about her family, María Martin actually seemed vulnerable. There was a sad exhaustion in her eyes, though her mouth was curved in a soft smile.

"Speaking of our families…my husband is determined that my children will be playing with guns. What did you say to him yesterday?"

The senator lost her smile.

"The truth as I see it, Emelda." The senator waved over a waiter. A young man with a thick mustache came running, "Julio, would you bring me and Madame Esquival two more coffees?

"Our nation is about to collapse from beneath us, Emelda. You're a smart woman, you can sense it just as well as I can. We are approaching a hungry moment, a vicious, carnivorous hour. I didn't tell your husband to arm your children, but I am glad he is."

"I don't want them learning to shoot."

María Martin laughed loudly, a dry wheezing thing that sent her into a coughing fit. Emelda could feel the eyes in the café on her, but she didn't look towards them. There was no telling who could hear her, no telling what these people who so readily armed their schoolchildren with rifles would make of a mother who disagreed.

"You sound so selfish. When I lost my daughter to cancer, I had no greater wish than for a gun that could shoot the rot out of her body. When my youngest had his accident, I nearly killed myself from grief. Imagine being so small, Emelda, in a place so dark and cold and so panicked you could barely form a thought, let alone scream for your mother. I nearly *killed myself* from the grief. But you've got a way to defend your children, a way for them to defend themselves. And you don't want them to have it why, because you're scared of guns?"

"What about your eldest, María, how do you feel about *his* death?"

The mustached waiter returned with their coffees. The smile on the senator's face was cold now, ready to unleash some cruel, spiteful remark. But first she made a show of sipping her coffee, taking it to her mouth and sighing heavily before lowering it with a shaking hand.

"Hugo was the only child of mine to die strong, and ready. I'm proud of him, and proud of the way he died."

Emelda couldn't stand her anger any longer. The words she spoke seemed to scrape against the back of her throat. "He died in a meaningless war that *you* started!"

"Nothing you say will deprive my son's life of meaning, Emelda!" Now María shook with something other than age. "You may refuse to give your brother's death any meaning, girl! But you will *not* accuse me of having loved a child who meant nothing. I won't have it! I left my child at the altar of our nation, the hardest thing a mother could ever have to do. I would do it again."

Emelda smirked. "You'd kill him all over again, would you?"

At that María Martin stood up, rising slowly and steadily as a plume of thick black smoke. She pointed to the door, slowly. "Leave."

Emelda nodded and stood up. "Before I go, I know you employed Antonio Villalobos. I don't know who helped him clean Casa Verde, but if I learn there are any keys out there in circulation and you didn't have them collected, I'll hold you responsible."

"I'm not the one deliberately inviting harm on your children, Emelda Salinas Esquival."

Emelda turned away from the senator, let her stew in her anger. The eyes of the café seemed like those of normal, concerned people, taken with a moment that would consume their gossip for the rest of the week. The wife of William Esquival, the madame of Casa Verde, had come down from the hill and fought with their senator. Truly, a thing to see.

But Emelda ignored them too and stepped out into the morning light. There were hours ahead to make herself heard by this entire city.

***

Outside of Casa Verde, William stooped down behind his son. Edward's feet were apart, both hands on the handle of his pistol. But his son had a pained expression on his face.

"You should concentrate, Edward, but there's no need to be afraid if you're careful. It is a weapon, but it is not a snake. It won't hurt you if you're careful."

He placed his hands on his son's shoulders and squeezed them gently. "You can be alert, but you can also relax."

"Right," Edward replied.

The morning had already faded from purple to bright blue. The sun was still behind them, the perfect light to see the pieces of paper William had nailed to the trees. Today he wasn't worried about his children hitting bull's-eyes; he just wanted them to learn to point and aim with more confidence than they had at the beginning of the day.

It seemed so peaceful; he could almost forget that this was to teach them to aim for a man's torso.

Torie seemed the most eager, strangely enthusiastic that she was going to learn to shoot. When William had explained to them that they were learning because one day they might be attacked, that they needed to be able to at least aim for the largest part of their attacker's body, Edward went a little pale. But not Torie, who only last week was afraid of the dark. She had wanted to go first, but William had convinced Edward to go, to show his sister how to shoot. William couldn't bring himself to put the gun in Téa's hands though, so his youngest sat on a bench behind them, blissfully unaware that anything was wrong or unusual.

The gun didn't tremble in his hands, but he seemed to hesitate.

William added, softly, "Once you do shoot, there is no taking it back. Remember that. You can't put the bullet back in the chamber. So take your time, breathe."

William had vowed that if he ever taught his son, let alone his daughter, to shoot, he would be kinder than his own father had been.

Ulysses Esquival. In retrospect, William had nothing to be terrified of in his father. He was a tall man, already balding even in William's earliest memories. He had been strong, though, wide-shouldered and with a lean athlete's muscles from daily exercise. But he was no giant, no monster. He'd walked with a limp, leaning on a cane from a childhood injury. If she had still been alive when his father started beating him, William believed his mother could have wrestled Ulysses to the ground and slit his throat. Sometimes he had fantasies about this, about his mother coming up from the grave as some righteous wraith to save him. At night he would imagine her crawling out of her tomb and visiting her husband as he lay in a drunken sleep. Would she whisper 'traitor' as she bit into him? Would she turn into an angel after, rising up the steps and taking her son with her into heaven?

Ulysses had been cruel, needlessly so. He'd envied his children, spat at their dreams, and physically struck them whenever he could. It drove his eldest son away, leaving William trapped with a bitter man who refused to die.

The last time William went shooting with his father, the man had insulted him mercilessly.

"You want to join the army? The army doesn't take goddamn *girls*. Ignore me and fire."

Then, right after taking his shot, Ulysses had struck his son across the back of his head with his cane. Surprised and disoriented, the blow had enough force to knock William off his feet. He rolled over on his back, and found the pistol in his hand pointed right at his father's chest.

As long as he lived, William would never forget the look on his father's face when he pointed a gun at him. A smug look, the look of years of hate finally bearing their expected fruit.

"*Go on then, Mr. Holcomb,*" his father had said. "*Do what soldiers do.*"

William understood then, finally, why his father hated his children so. He'd never believed they belonged to him at all.

Shortly thereafter, William's brother Edward came back. In his time away Edward had grown broad-shouldered, strong. He'd merely lifted their father by his neck and announced that William would be coming with him. That Ulysses would send monthly checks to pay for his education. Edward was a police officer now, and that meant that every cop in the neighborhood knew what Ulysses was. And no one, Edward growled into their father's ear, would suffer a man who beat his children.

William had never been so grateful to another human being in his life. So grateful that he joined the army and sent half of his paycheck home to Edward and his wife and child whenever he could. So grateful that he'd named his second son after his saintly older brother, who died before he could ever meet his second nephew.

When Edward fired, William wondered if he saw his brother's ghost in his youngest son. The sound of the bullet swallowed everything whole. From their nests in the forest, birds flew out in a panicked cloud.

"Good job, Edward. How do you feel?"

"I...I feel okay."

"Good. Do you see, it won't hurt you if you're careful."

"Yeah, yeah, I get it."

"Okay. Now." William only gave his son the pistol with one bullet loaded. William asked Torie to come see too, with little Téa trailing behind her. In truth, the presence of his youngest, who still couldn't read perfectly, did upset him. But if things were to become as bad as he feared, shooting might very well be more important. He showed them, carefully, the magazine well, the empty chamber. "Always inspect the chamber, but make sure you touch it too."

He loaded a full magazine in, undid the safety, and fired.

William had been a good but unexceptional shot in the army. His aim was reliable, and struck one of the paper targets towards the center. Had the target been a man, he would be stopped: if not killed, then bleeding profusely.

He then popped the magazine and handed it back to his son. "Your turn."

Edward, ever the fast learner, mimicked his father's motions as best as he could. When he fired towards a target, he actually hit it.

"Very good, son. Very good."

***

When Torie's turn came, she needed no prompting. She was faster than her brother, quickly loading the chamber and taking aim at the paper targets.

She had watched her father and Edward both while she held Téa's hand; she watched them and carefully looked at the position of the targets. She had mentally choreographed her aim, imagined how the gun would feel in her hands.

The first target was whoever had killed Alex. The bullet went through the paper and into the tree bark below.

The second target was the little girl in the woods, who'd scared them so badly yesterday.

The last target was the shadow, the looming monster that even now she believed she could see walking as some nearly invisible behemoth beneath the branches and leaves.

"Torie." Father said her name slowly behind her. "That was very good. You were very brave just now."

But Torie didn't feel brave at all. The gun made her more scared than ever. Light in her hands though it was, it was all the proof that her terror was real. That Alex was dead, that she and her family were encircled by monsters and that something even worse, something that had propelled Mother and Father to the worst argument they'd ever had, was coming next. Whatever that something was, she would be ready to meet it.

She handed the weapon back to her father. "Can we practice with the rifle next?" she asked.

The question seemed to take Father by surprise. "Maybe later in the week, honey. I really want you two to get comfortable with the pistol first. And besides, you're only going to need this if you're defending yourselves."

Father looked at all of them, carefully, making sure he made eye contact with each of them.

"If anything goes wrong, I want one of you to take this gun and hide. Hide with whoever you can. Your mother. Téa. You're protecting them too. That's what this is about, okay?"

"Yes sir," Edward answered. But there was a defeat in his voice, though Torie couldn't tell why.

"Yes," Torie recited back.

"Okay. I'm very proud of you both. I love you both."

Father was quiet a moment longer, looking towards the targets and then back to the kids. "Do you all need something to eat? It's going to be hot today and honestly, I could go back to sleep."

Téa shot her hand up quickly, laughing and asking for fruit in a sing-song voice.

"I'll stay out here, if that's all right," Torie answered. "I like the garden," she offered quickly, before her father could ask why.

"Okay. Edward, stay with your sister. Okay?"

"Yes sir."

Téa grabbed her father's hand and skipped ahead of him, pulling him back towards Casa Verde. Torie envied her little sister in that moment, who seemed young enough to forget the hardest things so quickly.

"Torie, we can't be out here," Edward said.

She didn't respond. Edward had always been the one who protected her, consoled her, who shushed her back to sleep when she was scared. He never minded when she was afraid, never complained about being a big brother. But he was made of bones and blood just as much as Alex had been. What if *he* needed protecting just as much as she did?

Torie did like the gardens; she hadn't lied to her father. She was tempted, even with all her heavy thoughts, to wander back to the hedge maze, to the walls of vibrant greens and blossoms with the hummingbirds weaving around them. She looked down at her shoes, though. Father had requested that they wear boots for shooting, and Torie had even put on pants. She didn't like wearing pants too much, because once she saw herself in the mirror and thought she looked too much like her brother. The thought of losing herself, of being confused with someone else, scared her just as much as anything.

"Torie."

"Eddie, you're so much smarter than me. I need to ask you a question."

"Okay?" he asked, confused.

"If they killed the Leite family in Margería, do you think we're safe here?"

"I…I don't know."

But he looked away from her.

"Eddie, don't lie to me."

He looked at her, pained, like he was suffering from a stomachache. He was quiet for a long time.

"No, no I don't think we're safe here." Then, looking away from her, he added softly: "I'm sorry."

"Eddie, what Father said about protecting everyone." On another day, she would have been in tears, trembling. But she had cried all of yesterday, all of last night. All her tears had left her, and in their place a resoluteness born from exhaustion filled her. And with it, a hate. A true, animal hate. She didn't know what the children in the forest were, or the shadow that loomed behind them. But she was going to know. "I'm going into the woods, Eddie."

"What?" He grabbed her, but she swatted him away forcefully. "Torie, no! It's dangerous."

But it was dangerous in the house. So dangerous that an intruder could come in and kill you in front of your whole family. There were no safe places left.

"It's dangerous everywhere, and if they're going to kill us, it may as well be now."

"Torie!"

But she was already walking away.

***

Christopher only grew more nervous as Antonio drove the carriage deeper into Rio Rojo. The city had its own charm, so much different from the stone and concrete jungle that was Margería. And yet, as he now understood, the local economy was not without its experts, its industries and its wealth.

"Antonio," he asked over the clomp of the horses' steps and the general murmurs of gossip and business along Rio Rojo's wooden sidewalks.

"Yes, Señor Christopher?"

"I understand that most of what I learned about Rio Rojo was propaganda. But, if there's all this money here, why do you still have dirt roads? And horses?"

Antonio laughed, his low voice warm and soothing as the last embers of a summer campfire. "Because everyone who lives in the devil's cradle understands the price paid for progress. Margería began life as a colonial throne, a careful Spanish thought, a distribution hub for a network of bloody colonies. It was never supposed to be a city, but even before the War of Unification, it had sprouted universities and seminaries like so many pompous fungi. The Founder was correct to keep it as the capital, but even in the early days the city's elites treated him like a swamp-dwelling barbarian.

"I have spent far more time in Margería than you have been alive, Señor Christopher. And I will tell you that I always feel sick in the city. It grew too quickly, so its water is dirty. The auto industry makes money, so the air is dank and grey. I always have a cough in the city, and stomach pains too.

"In Rio Rojo we understand that human flourishing does not mean you need autos. We live a little 'behind' our country to keep our water clean. Our lives richer."

"I see," Christopher said.

"I know you do. Having been lucky enough to make your friendship for only a few days, I can tell that you are a very intelligent young man. And with that, we have found your Miss Alma Sales."

Antonio had driven them to the public square. Though the roads around it were still dirt, the square itself was lined with neat, ivory-colored limestone bricks. Around it were wooden shops, bookstores and cafés. There was a running fountain, very much like the one in the gardens of Casa Verde. Instead of three dogs, though, it was only one, undoubtedly Dragón, who seemed to roar at the sky as water poured from her mouth like dragon's fire.

Sitting along the fountain's edge, Alma Sales drew with a large sketchbook in her lap. Seeing the blue ribbon in her short dark hair that matched the intensity of her eyes, Christopher felt something crawl up his stomach. For a moment, he panicked.

Antonio chuckled once more. "Be comfortable in your discomfort, Señor Christopher."

"What?"

"You would be surprised at how many men become so afraid of their own vulnerability. But a happy man knows he is vulnerable, and makes no serious effort to hide it. And Señor"—Antonio placed a hand on his shoulder—"a happy, honest man is far more pleasant company than a liar. A man can only appear tall so long if all he stands on are falsehoods. If you find her beauty terrifying, tell her."

"Tell her!? That I'm *scared*?"

"Yes, young man! *Tell her*. And then, when she assuages your fear, you may thank me."

And with that, Antonio shooed him out of the carriage, laughing uproariously as he drove the horses away.

On the square, Christopher felt impossibly alone. His wrists were cold. Every other person faded away until there was only Alma. In her blue dress. Rifle slumped at her side.

His feet felt like stone, but he moved them anyway. His throat was dry. His face hot.

When he stood before her, he found the courage to ask.

"What are you drawing?"

She looked up at him, for a moment puzzled. Recognizing him, she smiled, and motioned for him to sit beside her.

He sat close to her, the warmth of her side touching his.

"I come here for inspiration. Rio Rojo isn't a backwater, but it is small enough. If I sit here for a few hours each week, I come to know everyone in the city."

She pointed to a man sitting on a metal bench outside a bookstore, a brown paper bag next to him. He was a young man, with thin hair and a lean face with sharp, angular features. In her drawing, it seemed that Alma had captured his appearance nearly perfectly: the thin rims of his glasses, the paleness of his eyes.

"You're very good," he added eagerly.

She smiled, and the butterflies in his stomach seemed to calm. "Thank you, Christopher. What are you doing in the city to-day?"

For a moment he thought of an excuse, an attempt to escape the awkwardness. Then he remembered what Antonio said. "Well, I was hoping I would see you."

She stopped drawing and looked at him closely. Her face was close to his now, pensive and concerned.

Then she laughed. "Don't you think I'm a little...*intense?*"

"Y-yes. But you're also pretty."

"Only 'pretty'?" she asked, her white teeth glinting mischievously.

"Beautiful!" he sputtered out, louder than he meant. "*Terrifyingly* beautiful."

This seemed to stop her. The mischief, the concern, the playfulness all left her. Now her mouth, so close to his, only formed a soft 'o' in surprise. She withdrew from him, sighed, and looked ahead.

The panic returned. "I'm sorry," he began. "I know I'm creepy, I know. I can go, I'll leave you alone."

"No." She touched his shoulder gently. "The men in this town, particularly the young ones. They can run, shoot, they can do all of these things. But I don't believe I have ever met anyone half so bold as you."

And with that, all the panic left him. He no longer felt uneasy, unwanted. He wanted to lean on her shoulder, to thank her from the bottom of his heart. How good those words made him feel!

They sat quietly for a moment, watching the town pass them by.

"Well," she ventured. "Your hope has come true. You've seen me. Now what?"

***

Edward was still trying to convince his sister against going into the forest.

He was scared, and he had every reason to be.

Edward was young, but was always doted on as being "smart for his age." He was more comfortable talking to adults than kids his age, who were too loud and too rough for him to really understand. Even though they gravitated towards him, talking with his peers was alienating, so much so that more often than not he merely kept quiet when spontaneous conversations formed around him in school.

It was easier to read a book, or to exercise in private, than it was to talk about comics or Tarzan. When he did try, he used words other kids didn't know, and they looked at him warily, sensing that he was so far removed from them that he wasn't approachable at all.

Edward knew horror from stories. He knew about supernatural terror, demons and ghosts. But he never once believed in them. Even when he was little, he'd closed his bedroom door so he could sleep, confident that nothing would change in the dark.

But he had never been as afraid as he was in the woods outside of Casa Verde.

"Please, Torie," he called ahead.

Edward needed to be a big brother. Torie was his best friend. He only understood this now, when losing her seemed more than a possibility. As far back as he could remember, she had been there too. And though he couldn't talk to other kids, he could always talk to her. He knew she didn't understand, but she would listen. He loved that about her. He loved how deeply she felt things, how excited butterflies made her.

Edward needed his little sister. He wasn't willing to lose her, and tried to catch up with her so he could pull her back towards the house.

But Torie was resolute now.

She nearly ran through the woods, only pausing to push aside branches, thorns and vines. The air so far in the forest was thick with wet leaves, still wet from the nightly rain. The trees came together in an interconnected curtain of branches and leaves. The dirt beneath them was rich, and anything could grow as long as it was strong enough to reach the sunlight. But the tangling of vines and branches gradually seemed to swallow the sun and sky, and the green world began to filter into grey.

They couldn't be that far from Casa Verde, but already the forest was overtaking them.

In every direction he looked, Edward only saw walls of vegetation, moss hanging from tree limbs in green-grey funeral veils. The birds only grew louder, but their singing seemed to rise and fall in screams. The underbrush whipped him as he sped up, desperate not to lose sight of his sister.

"Torie!"

"Eddie, shush," she hissed back. She held a finger up behind her, and Edward stopped in his tracks. He had never seen her so commanding before, and the sight scared him. "I see something."

His stomach fell. He felt cold. Ghosts sometimes sucked all the heat out of life. That's what he'd read once. But he'd also read that cold is a natural response to terror, a bodily reflex in the face of stress and anxiety.

"Is it one of them?" he whispered back. His voice wasn't trembling, but it was dry and raspy.

"No," she responded, still coldly. "I think it's a graveyard."

She took his wrist and led him forward. The foliage thinned, and the sunlight came back into view. He wanted nothing more than to run.

"Torie!"

But she was stronger than him. Somehow, she'd become stronger than him.

The clearing was green and glittering, with unhindered sunlight that could reach the forest floor. Flowers, every bit as vibrant and brilliant as those in the garden, grew wild, curling around each other in a fight towards the sun. The hummingbirds darted along them, moving so fast between the red and yellow blossoms that they seemed to have no shape at all, but were rather flashes of green light.

The tombstones were neatly arranged, though colored black by rain and time. Worn, Edward could still make out the names. He stopped at one.

"Elizabeth Salazar," he read out loud.

There was no other information. No date of birth, death or title.

He frowned and scanned the other stones for names. Every one had the name "Salazar."

"Who do you think they were?" A sense of fear had finally returned to Torie's voice.

"I don't know," Edward responded, swallowing his own fear once more. "Maybe they were the owners of this land before Holcomb? Maybe this is a family cemetery?"

But if that was true, the ground would have been better kept. There would have been gates, more ornate stones. Even before Casa Verde, Edward knew landowners had been wealthy people. And he had never heard, not once, of a family that kept its private graveyards secret. In Margería, private mausoleums were a show of wealth, and he couldn't imagine things would be different in Rio Rojo.

He stopped at one stone, smaller than the rest. "Augustus *Holcomb?*"

Edward was more than familiar with his great-grandfather's family tree. There was no 'Augustus.'

Torie gasped.

At the edge of the woods, the children were watching.

In the shadows they were clearer, giving their own light like faint fairy glow. Their skin was pale, like the underbelly of some cave-dwelling serpent or slug. The hair on their heads was mangled and messy, lodged with branches and leaves from the forest. But their clothes were clean: neat white linen that clung to them like nightgowns.

Seeing them so close now, Edward knew they had no eyes. Instead, something cavernous, dark and hollow looked back at him.

There were so many of them, peeking out from between the trees and encircling them on all sides. Fifty? One hundred?

Edward's stomach twisted into a knot.

"Are you a brother?"

The speaker resembled a young boy, somewhere between five and six. He stepped out of the forest and towards Edward, shining like a pearl in the sun.

He couldn't move. The boy came closer now. There was a horrible smell on him, a sour, sharp scent.

When he spoke next, Edward could see his sharp teeth and smell his breath. It was like something had died inside him. "Are you a brother?"

He didn't understand. What was the boy asking? "I…"

"We're all brothers. All sisters."

And at that moment, for the first time in his life, Edward wanted to die. The thought came so clearly to him, rising above his terror: "*I want to die.*" This was too scary, he was too afraid. He didn't want to imagine what could come next, let alone live through it. Why wasn't the world going dark? Why wasn't his life flashing before his eyes? Why was he still here when the boy took his hand in his own? Why could he hear Torie's panicked breathing? Why did his lungs still breathe? Would his body not listen? Why?

The back of the boy's hand was on his face. It was cold, and smelled like the top of a riverbed.

"D-don't touch him!"

The boy turned his empty eyes, and Edward's followed. Torie was standing close by. She'd picked up a large branch somewhere, something so big that she winced when she lifted it above her head.

"Don't touch him or I'll hurt you."

The boy seemed puzzled. They all did.

Scanning the forest, Edward found now malice in their faces. Their expressions were just as vacant as their dark eyes, mouths pulled tight in silent "hmmms."

More stepped outward into the graveyard. There were boys, girls. Some very young, holding the hands of the taller ones as if they were little siblings. Others were older, with pale, scraggly mustaches just like Christopher's.

"Sister, you can't hurt us. No one can."

"We're past hurt now," a little girl with moss tangled in her hair answered. "Past pain."

"What...what do you want from us?" Edward ventured to ask, barely able to speak over his terror.

The boy removed his hand from Edward's cheek and smiled. There was something awful there, but Edward couldn't put it into a coherent thought. "To show you something."

"Something important," the little girl answered.

"Something *very* important," the boy affirmed.

"Come and see!" a boy replied enthusiastically.

"Yes, yes, please do!" the little girl responded.

The voices from the forest joined them, a goading sing-song chorus of soft sighs and laughs, the sounds of mothers reading to their children, the songs of children sighing.

"If...if we go"—Edward found his voice returning because it needed to—"Will you leave us alone? Will you promise to not hurt us?"

Again the children seemed puzzled and confused. "We already said you can't hurt us. Of course we can't hurt you!"

"Why?" Edward replied. "Why can't you hurt us? Why can't we hurt you?"

"You can't hurt what you love. It's against the rules."

The children laughed, as if what had been said was so obvious it was funny.

The boy ran ahead. "Come and see!" he called back.

"Come and see!" the girl called back too.

Edward turned to Torie. Only yesterday she had been crying. Crying all day. Last week she had been so scared to leave Margería that she'd never left Edward's side. Now she looked afraid, but also determined; she was glaring at the children, squinting into the woods as if looking for something else. She caught Edward's look and smiled, the only thing she could do.

The smile woke something up in him, and he held his hand out for her. When she took it, he felt brave again.

They followed the children into the woods.

Walking through the trees, there were so many more. In the darkness they were fully visible, and seemed to flank them on all sides like soldiers. Some walked beside them; others climbed the branches. Still others chased each other, laughing wildly and loudly. The only word Edward could think of was "swarm." These children were a swarm.

They paid no mind to the branches that would cut or bruise them, but neither did they cut or bruise. The twigs and underbrush seemed to just break against them, but the children merely ignored them. Edward could see no blood on them, nothing breaking out from beneath their pale skin.

Torie squeezed his hand tight.

They walked with the children for minutes. Edward realized, hopelessly, that he was not sure where they were. They were being led somewhere, and the children seemed to know where they were going, but he and Torie would have no idea how to get back to Casa Verde. He tried to concentrate on finding landmarks, trees and flowers that he could use to find his way back, but the children unnerved him, and he found concentration to be nearly impossible.

"Hello!" one child's voice called out.

Others enthusiastically joined in. "Hello! Hello!"

Torie squeezed Edward's hand so tight it hurt.

There was something with them between the trees. Something dark that eclipsed the light of the glowing children, so dark, so indistinct that it seemed like a formless cloud. Then, at another moment, it appeared to have legs. In another, claws. Edward believed he could see the form of a massive black hound, a lumbering thing that rose to the forest canopy. Yellow eyes bearing down on them.

"What...what is that?"

Torie was speechless, but she walked forward nonetheless.

"Our good mother!" one child chimed.

"Our blessed father!" another chimed back.

"Our beautiful everything!" the chorus rang out.

The children continued singing, and the shadow walked with them.

The cicadas, the birds joined in on the chorus. Then it seemed the shadow, whatever it was, lent its own voice as well. The sound was horrible, a low rumbling growl mixed with the soft tenor of a mother's voice. At this the children shouted and giggled, darting wildly about. Some answered the shadow's voice with howling, by getting down on all fours and running between the trees like beasts. Others snarled at each other, playfully biting like dogs who knew full well they wouldn't bleed, no matter how hard they bit.

Edward squeezed Torie's hand back.

The sound of Rio Sangría began to rise above them all. The water began as a gurgle, and rose to a roar.

Light began to pour from in between the trees.

The bank of the river was a primal, beautiful place. The red water cut the land as an ever-flowing wound, and long trees extended their branches above the river to catch some of its cold moisture. On the other side of the river, only jungle stood watch. Edward knew no one lived on the other side of the river, that Rio Rojo was the capital of the state and one of the only inhabited cities. But there on the far bank of the river, he imagined he could see them. Even *more* of them. Legions of hollow eyes. He strained his sight, but couldn't be sure if the light he saw came from the far bank, or merely from the sun reflecting off the water.

He and Torie stood at the bank. Behind them, the children stood silent.

He turned to them and found their faces serene. He searched for the thing that walked with them, for the shadow. He couldn't see it, but felt it. Felt it with the same certainty with which he felt the sun on his skin. It was in the woods, beneath every tree.

A woman rose out of the river.

Her hair was short and blond. Her eyes were green and glowing.

She rose up from the deepest part of the river, and swam across its fastest currents as if it were nothing. Reaching the shallows, she stood tall. Impossibly tall. She crouched down before them. Her hand ran along the back of Edward's neck. Her touch was wet and cool, her smile calm and gentle.

She placed her other hand on the small of his back and embraced him, pushing him into herself. It was like he was being cradled, but he couldn't breathe. She wasn't choking him, but he couldn't breathe. He was frozen again, too scared to offer any fight.

The woman walked backwards into the water.

The water rose up to his feet.

Somewhere, Torie was screaming.

***

William watched his daughter greedily tear into a bowl of fruit. They ate in a smaller kitchen in Casa Verde, a room that William believed had once been the servants' dining quarters. There was a simple wooden table, a cabinet of plain dishes and cutlery, and a window that looked down towards the city of Rio Rojo.

The local farmers produced some of the best pineapples he had ever tasted in his life, and now Téa smacked at her lips as sour juice dribbled out of the side of her mouth.

He gently put a napkin to her cheek. For a moment she stopped, as if confused. But when he grinned at her, she grinned back.

William missed when his other children had been so easy to please. Christopher was once little just like her. Christopher used to be unable to walk, let alone speak. He was once a soft, bald thing who merely cried and slept. Once, he had even been small enough to sleep in one of his father's arms.

William had adjusted to child-rearing faster than he believed he would. He would stay up with his children when they were small, even bringing them to his office when he could so he could rock their cribs with his foot as he read report after report after report. He often wondered if he'd been greedy in those days, if he took all of his infant children's time for himself and didn't share enough of it with Emelda.

Emelda had always intended to go back to practicing medicine, and for the years between Christopher and Edward, she had done exactly that. She'd served as a doctor in a nearby government clinic, tending to people with the same mercy and care she allotted her husband and child. But when Edward came, and Torie thereafter, Emelda lost interest in resuming a career.

"I'm tired of only seeing hurting people, William. Does that make me selfish?"

Emelda had always been averse to suffering, yet always the first one to rush to alleviate it. But his wife had grown tired. She wasn't selfish; at least, he had never thought so.

If either of them was selfish, it was him. He knew it was wrong to announce that the children would learn to hold guns, learn to be soldiers. It was a disservice to her, to make a decision so against her preferences and without her input. He knew it was cruel, and he hated himself for it.

He hated the idea of losing his family even more.

And again, his thoughts turned to Ulysses Esquival. William wondered if his father was still alive, after all these years. His children had never known their grandfather, though Ulysses did try once. He came to the door of their home while Emelda lay sleeping with Christopher.

The old man had seemed so pathetic and sick, far thinner and far more grey than the man who beat him as a child. For a moment William had even entertained the notion that his father had changed, that being so estranged from his sons that he wasn't even allowed to attend his eldest's funeral had broken him. In that moment, when the old man was unable to meet his gaze, William had been ready to embrace his father.

But then he spoke.

"I deserve to see my grandchild."

'Deserve.' William had laughed at his father and closed the door abruptly.

His mother's family had been no better. Being in the house, he remembered his final visit more clearly, or at least he thought he did: aunts, uncles, and cousins of a dying nobility who pretended they were kings and queens of the world, even as their fortune and home rotted around them. People who held contests about which one of them most resembled Thomas Holcomb, who stood next to his portraits and announced, "Well, you see now, I resemble the devil himself!"

Calling Holcomb 'the devil' had terrified William, and made him question whether he had the devil's blood in him, if he was human at all.

It was true William had pursued a career in politics, but he hated aristocracy, hated the abuse and horror that nobility bred. He wanted to be a good father, an egalitarian husband. And in making a decision without Emelda, he'd betrayed every one of those desires.

But he wasn't as bad as his father. Or as bad as the Holcomb family, unable to step out from the legacy of an ancestor many of them had never even met.

He was going to save his family. And when they were safe, he would apologize.

Téa held out her bowl. "Papa, more?"

"You sure are hungry, little thing."

"Can I have berries, please?" she asked with a smile.

William always bowed to the whims of his smiling children, who so easily wielded the keys to his heart. He handed her a bowl of blackberries, which she took quickly from his hands.

Idly, he wondered what appliances in the old servants' kitchen were still functional. There was a refrigerator, which he'd found in remarkable working order, but also a radio. Most of the radios he had encountered in the house were functional, and on the national radio station he was able to catch the latest, most gruesome news. The latest broadcast warned that there communist guerillas in the devil's cradle. He wondered if they knew he was here, if he would be killed just as Katrina Leite had been for being "a traitor to the revolution." He hoped he could convince them to leave his family be, that there would be no need to hurt them.

He thought of Elías Pasqual, and his classes on theology. The bloody priest had a hunger even then, though in those days it was mostly for young, pretty students. In the classroom, Pasqual made William uncomfortable. There was something particularly horrifying about seeing a priest who had never killed speak so willingly and enthusiastically of the idea. Even then his lectures and sermons had all the smatterings of a call to arms. For a moment, William wondered if there was a kindred spirit there, a man so dedicated to fighting injustice that he found a way to reconcile the supposed differences between Marx and Christ.

But then, William raised his hand in class, and asked the preacher about these tensions.

He had expected a quote from the sermon on the mount, a compassionate redemption of the idea of revolution, a marriage of gospel and praxis that would be found in action and reform.

Instead, Pasqual quoted the gospel.

"Do not assume I have to bring peace to the earth; I have come not to bring peace, but a sword. For I have come to turn a man against his father, a daughter against her mother."

William reached for the radio, terrified that he might hear that Pasqual and his followers might have further encircled them. He turned the dial, switching through jazz, static, and finally into the national news.

"We will bring you the latest news when we can." The announcer seemed frantic, panting and speaking far more quickly than he normally did. "We are told that tanks have been sighted outside the presidential palace and the congress. Soldiers are storming the offices of our sister station."

William went cold.

"I have been told that our barricade has been broken down. It has been a pleasure to serve as your host for two decades. Long live our Republic, and good luck."

From there, silence.

Then the unmistakable sound of gunfire.

"Ladies and gentlemen, do not panic." The voice was fast, firm and deep. "The glorious army of the Antiochan Republic has heard your call. For the autonomy and freedom of the people, and with unrelenting patriotism, we have mobilized to retake our nation from the Marxist threat. We advise you to stay inside your residences. We will have further announcements for you on this station.

"Long live our Republic."

***

Christopher wasn't aware he could experience so many emotions at once. He was happy, to be sure. Happy, nervous, scared and more. Alma took him from the fountain and into a nearby café. He was immediately taken aback by the place: not because of anything remarkable about the décor, but rather because every patron seemed to be a high school student. In the entire two stories, separated by a metal spiral staircase, teenagers took books off shelves, lounged on chairs, and held soft conversations over tea and coffee.

Alma led him to a table by a tall window facing the town square and beckoned him to sit in a red armchair.

She sat opposite from him and smiled. "Did you think taking a girl for coffee was the safest choice?"

That made him blush. Everything she said made his face feel hot. A week ago his instinct would have been to get mad and leave, assuming that she was teasing and laughing at him. That she would tell jokes about him to her friends.

Now, though, he simply laughed back when he blushed. "I did. Is there somewhere else you'd like to be?"

"In truth, no. Your instinct was right. Coffee is a way of life in this country, particularly in Rio Rojo. And certainly, I need it."

"Antonio Villalobos told me you were one of his best students," he responded. "And you're class president. I imagine that takes a lot of work."

"It does. But I'm a natural at it." She chuckled. "The coffee helps, though."

A waiter came and approached them. He seemed to know Alma, as his response was "Hello again," rather than "May I take your order?" And somehow Christopher believed he had also seen this man before, that there was something familiar in his round face and patchy beard.

"Hello, Sampson." Alma smiled back. She turned to Christopher, "How do you drink your coffee?"

"I—"

"There's really no need to be embarrassed." She placed a gentle hand on his knee. His heart shot into his throat. "Some men drink their coffee black. Others don't. It's hardly a 'status symbol' worth choking over. Don't you believe it would be more embarrassing coughing all over yourself than ordering something sweeter?"

She was direct. Was she always so direct?

"I do take mine black, though," he answered.

Her eyes went wide, and her mouth dropped into an "o." She laughed. "Then it seems that *I* have embarrassed *myself.*"

Alma asked Sampson for two black coffees. After he left, Alma sighed. "I'm sorry. I was trying to be nice, but I think I may have teased you too much then."

"No, it's okay. I understand. After yesterday, I know why you would think that I needed sugar in my coffee."

"Why is that?"

"Well, I wasn't a very good shot."

"Have you ever needed to shoot before?" she asked.

Sampson returned with their coffees, in neat gold-rimmed porcelain cups. Christopher brought his to his lips and sighed. Thick, bitter. "I've shot on trips with my father before."

"That's not what I mean," Alma elaborated. She leaned back in her chair and stared at him intently.

"You grew up in Margería. What did you need to know? How to find your way across a sprawling city. How to haggle. Which neighbors are dangerous, which are not. How to use your fists, certainly. But did you ever need a rifle? I would imagine not.

"Christopher, there is no shame in someone not knowing something they have never needed before. Certainly, there is no shame in not being perfect at something when they're just starting. I don't know who gave you such toxic notions, but perhaps you would be better off abandoning them."

He had never heard such things said before. He remembered when he was young, how it seemed that everything came easily to him. Running, writing and reading. But as he got older, it felt his emotions would often overpower him. He couldn't stand struggling with things he didn't understand, things that didn't come naturally to him. And he watched his brother, growing quickly from a little boy to a handsome man, quickly master all the world could throw at him. It made Christopher angry, volatile. Made him hate himself.

"Wow," was all he said. "I don't think anyone has ever said something that kind to me before."

"When I was a little girl—" Alma's eyes turned to the people walking on the square. "My little brother drowned in the river. He was a strong swimmer. So was my father. But somehow he drowned, and somehow my father couldn't save him. Since then, I've learned that too much of life is wasted on not telling people how you feel."

"I'm…so sorry about losing your little brother."

"Me too." She turned back to him. "Are you a good older brother?"

He hadn't thought about that question for some time. He'd watched Edward be a better big brother to his little sisters and, like anything else he struggled being good at, Christopher just abandoned being a big brother entirely. He didn't know when it happened, or why. He used to be attentive, at least more so.

"No," he answered. "No, I don't think I am, to be honest."

"Well." Alma seemed to frown. "That will have to change, don't you think?"

He looked at her. She was so sure of herself, so confident.

"Just like you'll need to learn to shoot better, you'll have to learn to be a better big brother."

"How did you learn to shoot so well?" he asked, eager to take the topic of conversation away from himself.

"It's like I said. I *needed* to."

"Okay, then, why did you *need* to?"

"The devil's cradle has birthed more warriors than any region of our country. The first tribes to fight against the Spanish came from this dirt. Then the war against the English. Finally, the War of Unification."

"So 'it's tradition'?"

She smiled sharply. "Yes. But more than tradition." Her smile turned mischievous, and she motioned for him to lean over the table. She cupped her hand to his ear. "There are communist spies everywhere. And…there's only one thing to do with them."

His stomach fell.

Her smile widened.

"Sampson?" Alma waved their waiter back over. "Could you come and bring us something to eat? Something small to share, maybe?"

When the waiter came back to the table, Christopher finally recognized him from the paper target he'd shot at yesterday. The man whose face he'd put a bullet through.

Before he could say anything, the café grew quiet. The students put down their books. Several waiters dropped their trays.

Over the radio, a loud, booming voice proclaimed: "At this time it is unknown if President Ambert is dead, but our troops are fighting to reach him. Citizens, put your faith in your armed forces. Put faith in your sons."

He turned to Alma, whose smile never left.

***

Emelda needed to find her son.

She had been at the town library, going through books on the Holcomb family, when she heard a man yelling.

"The capital! The army has taken the capital!"

She needed to get back home. She needed to find Christopher. She needed to hold her husband. Her daughters. She needed a world she could control, a place where she could keep everyone important to her between her arms.

The crowds on the street hardly seemed like people to her as she ran. They were mannequins: still, transfixed and silent as the world around them changed. The entire town of Rio Rojo strained to listen to their radios, ceased drinking their coffees or driving their horses.

Where would he be? Where would Antonio have taken him?

They couldn't wait for their own coachman. They would need to find some quicker way back to Casa Verde. It was okay; she had money and would pay anything to create her safe, small world.

"Christopher!?" she called out to no one in particular. She didn't trust these people. She didn't trust this town. "Christopher?"

Where was he? Where was he?

She turned into the main square, to the fountain of Thomas Holcomb's dog. People crowded the cafés and restaurants, their eyes fixed on whatever radios they could find. The only sound other than the running was the occasional whisper of "God protect us."

"Christopher!?"

"Mother!"

Christopher was in the entryway of a restaurant. There was a girl at his side.

"Baby!"

Emelda hadn't called him "baby" for years, but he was her baby. In that moment he was her everything. He was all of the world she could hold and she held him tight, throwing her arms around him.

"Thank God." She was not a praying woman, unsure if she believed in God or not. But she prayed now, thanked him now. "Baby, we need to get back home."

"Mother—"

"We need to be with your father."

"It's okay," the girl by Christopher said.

He turned to her.

"Your family is the most important thing in the world. Especially right now."

"Okay," Christopher stammered back to her.

"We'll see each other later, I promise."

Emelda thanked the girl too. Even in this unquiet moment, she felt some indistinct power this child had. Some hold over her son. Was it love?

"Do you need to come with us too?" Emelda asked the girl. "Do you have a safe place to be right now?"

The girl smiled gently, as if attempting to calm Emelda. "Thank you, Mrs. Esquival. But I promise you there is no one safer in Rio Rojo than me.

"We'll protect your family," the girl added, uninvited.

Emelda merely nodded and took her son by the wrist.

"Mother." He shook her off his wrist and instead grabbed her own. "We're going to make it back. Okay? We're going to make it back."

Yes.

Yes.

They would make it back. They would make it back and everything would be okay.

***

William bolted out into the garden, bellowing for his children.

He returned to the shooting range, ran through the maze. Where were they?

"Torie! Edward!" He yelled until his voice went hoarse.

They'd gone into the woods. He wanted to deny it, because if they were in the woods then it would take him hours to find them. In that time, the world could change forever. They needed to be with him. He needed to be able to cradle them, to promise everything would be okay. If he could promise them, he would have to make that promise come true. He was a father. A good father. Good fathers made the world safe for their kids.

Good fathers kept their kids safe.

Finally, he saw them.

Torie was supporting Edward, his arm draped across her shoulders. The two of them were wet, soaking wet. He didn't care. He didn't have any impulse to scold them, to ask where they had been.

He ran to his children. "We need to go inside."

William forgot how strong he could be when he needed to be. Both of them were in his arms now, and he ran faster than he ever had in the war. He ran through the gardens, his children cradled and safe. He set them down.

"Father—"

"Kids." He bent down to them. Something was wrong. Torie had a distant look, something cold and nearly empty. A look he had seen before, but never on a child. "Kids," he panted.

Edward looked defeated. Broken.

Something was wrong.

But the voice over the radio rose above his thoughts.

"We can now confirm that President Ambert has been killed.

"This is a sad moment, Antiochans. But your army is with you."

***

Dispatch #113, from Elías Pasqual

Children of Antioch,

Do not mistake your faith to be a faith of passivity. This was the lie of your fathers, told to their fathers before them by men who would be fathers to us all. But they are no good father, no good shepherd who leaves no lamb behind. They are merciless things, meaning to ground the stray lamb to the ground. To press for blood so that you and your children will wade in it up to your waists.

Do not mistake your faith to be a faith of waiting. For it was the Lord who said, "I am come to send on fire the earth; and what will I, if it be already kindled?"

"Fire."

Do not mistake your faith to be a faith of kindness. For it was the Lord who said, "Do not assume I have to bring peace to the earth; I have come not to bring peace, but a sword. For I have come to turn a man against his father, a daughter against her mother."

The Lord our Holy God comes bringing swords and fire!

"And another horse went forth. It was bright red, and its rider was granted permission to take peace from the earth and to make men slay one another. And he was given a great sword."

Bright. And Red.

Your faith is a faith of fire. A faith of action. A faith of liberation and of justice. As the Lord God drove the tax collectors from the temple so too shall we drive the vipers from our temple! For too long you lambs have suffered under the yokes of your lying mothers, your vile fathers, all too content to give faith in God over to faith in capital. But the land barons, the swine, they are all too content themselves. To ruin God's earth. To strangle children. You, who by some miracle have survived their greed. The greed that has taken a brother, a mother, perhaps it did indeed nearly take you!

Well I say to you that it is no miracle that you were brought from that greed. Rescued. Saved.

It is not some miracle that you stand before me today. No. It is the will of our Lord God!

The Lord has come to light a fire. But it is already lit. Then we, his children, will raise the flames higher. We, his children, will bring the sword.

Their blood will cover our rivers. Their blood will flow to the salty sea. The last one we hang will be the one who sells the rope. And we will not know apologies. Not for this holy terror. This swift, divine justice!

PART II

nd for a moment the nation stood still. In the country-side they could hear the ash and smoke fall on the capital. The wind carried whispers, forming words that no still-human mouth ever could. A pronouncement in silence wove its way between the trees as it echoed from the streets of the cities and wrapped around the highest peaks.

Change, irrevocable and absolute, had arrived. And in the distant roar, they knew that there was more to come.

REGROUPING

Christopher would not let go of his mother's hand.

Behind them, the town of Rio Rojo grew more still and more silent. The silence was electric, full of anticipation and anxiety. Only the slow, methodical clomp of the horse pulling their coach up the hill and the occasional whispers of the bewildered coachman filled the silence.

Before pulling the poor man aside and throwing money at him, Christopher and his mother heard one of the radios announce that President Ambert had been killed.

Christopher felt the grief, the fear like a blow across the back of his head. Christopher Ambert had been his godfather, a frequent family guest long before he had ever been a presidential contender. Christopher didn't have much in common, he felt, with the man he was named for. But he was an important man who'd officiated his parents' wedding, taught his father in the university where he was a professor, and had served as mayor of Margería, governor of the Central Department, and ultimately president.

But now all Christopher could think of was the man's genuineness, his authentic, real happiness and kindness. About how he had never once spoken to Christopher like a child, but always like an equal, even when he was barely learning to walk. How he would always let Christopher finish his thoughts, even when they were incomplete and half-formed. How he would always, when a guest in their home, ask Christopher how he was and show that he actually cared.

It was not uncommon for Christopher to receive a letter from his godfather after his visits. Dr. Ambert's letters always mentioned how pleased he was at his godson's "progress," and even made reference to the matter of their conversations. Though he only sometimes offered advice, Dr. Ambert always made Christopher feel like he was heard.

But in his death, Christopher had lost far more than his godfather. He'd lost his president.

Antioch lost its president.

The world felt unanchored, freed from any certainty to keep it calm and still.

"Mother," he said to break the silence.

His mother had been as quiet and still as the rest of the universe. Where she was once so panicked, so alarmed and desperate to get back home, it now seemed she was imagining herself somewhere else. Maybe it was greedy, pulling her back here where the sky was falling, but he needed her.

She looked at him. There were no false smiles offered. No gentle reassurances. Just the look of a person seeing only bleak horizons. Only dark futures.

"Dr. Ambert introduced me to your father, you know?"

Christopher did know, but he let his mother tell the story.

"I was getting ready for my medical career. I had dated in college, sure, but I'd never been in love. Truth be told," she laughed—not out of humor, but because this part of the story *needed* a laugh—"I believe I had a crush on my professor of politics. Dr. Ambert always had a charisma about him. He was such a good teacher that I nearly abandoned my medical studies for him my first year of university. But he dissuaded me, and set me back on the right course. I stayed in touch with him, though, and it was in a walk in to his office hours that I met your father.

"'My dear Emelda.'" Her impression of the president was to raise her hands to her chest and move them wildly. Dr. Ambert had a tendency to "speak from his chest," a strategy William Esquival had adopted early into his political career. "'Please meet the most incredible young man, Mr. William Esquival. Now, I'm afraid we are in the process of divesting young Mr. Esquival of his...military mind. However, I believe he is one of the single brightest students to ever visit with me. If you would, though, take him off my hands. Yes, boy, you're bothering me, though I would be lying if I said I did not enjoy it. However, I believe your thoughts would become clearer in the company of a more agile mind.'

"At the moment, I was furious with my professor. Who was he to unload some boy on me? You have to understand, too, how biased students were against soldiers. We thought they were backward, unlearned, that they would always have to play catch-up to us. Who was this old man, whom I believed a dear friend, to foist me upon a dullard? But your father was no dullard, and though I can't remember what we talked about that day over coffee and cake, I can tell you that even now I remember how my smile tingled when I left."

"He was a good man," Christopher offered.

At the "was," something broke in Mother's eyes. Wherever she had been, she was back with him now, and the tears came like cold water bursting from the dirt.

He moved beside her and let her lean on his shoulder, and ran his hand through her hair.

Just as she had once done for him.

The coachman arrived at Casa Verde, and Christopher let his mother lean on him still. Her steps were slow, uneven.

"Thank you," he called to the coachman behind him. The man said nothing in reply, probably just as eager to return to his own home, his own family.

Even the Casa Verde grounds now seemed emptier, stiller. The birds from the forest seemed to be softer, the blue sky more impassive. And all the flowers, gardens, the wall of ivy along the side of the house, all of it was the picture of a home, a frozen photo, rather than part of any living world.

William burst through the door. "Emelda, son!"

He barked the words. Their only meaning was that he saw them, that he needed them. They weren't questions, but pronouncements: "I need you. I need you."

Emelda lifted herself from her son. "He's dead, William! He's dead!"

"I know."

Watching his parents, Christopher now realized how powerless they truly were.

***

Torie had managed to get Edward away from the woman in the water.

The children tried to hold her back, but they weren't strong.

She threw them off, struck at the woman, tried to tear into her with her nails. But her skin wouldn't break. They had fought in the water until she wrenched the woman's arm off of Edward and ran from the water.

The children didn't chase them, but they were quiet now. They seemed to make a path for her, standing in long lines on either side. All through the woods, empty eyes had stared at them.

When Torie saw her father, she was ready to be called a liar. She was ready for his cool hand to touch her head and feel for a fever. She was ready, because she would drag him to the water. She was ready, because Edward would tell him too.

But now, surrounded by everyone else, Torie had nothing to say.

The Esquival family sat together in a living room furnished with old, ornate furniture. She and Edward had changed out of their wet clothes, but they still hadn't managed to talk to each other. All through the house, their father had turned on every radio he could find. With Mother, they walked the hallways frantically, searching for any update they could find.

For the first time in a long time, Christopher sat next to Torie. He didn't say anything, but pulled her into him with one arm. She'd forgotten how strong her older brother felt. How safe she felt at his touch.

Téa sat on the floor. She knew something was wrong, but it wasn't clear that she understood what. Every now and then she would ask a question, sometimes the same question.

"Why was the army in the capital?"

"I don't know," Christopher answered for them all.

"Now the army is fighting itself?"

"I don't know."

"What happens now?"

"..."

"What happens now?"

"I don't know," Christopher answered, again for them all.

Eventually, Mother and Father returned to the living room. Whatever anger had been between them was meaningless now. They had both been crying; Torie could see it in the red skin around their eyes and hear it in their sniffling. But their parents tried to be brave now.

Torie could be brave too.

But it was so hard. Her chest hurt. Her stomach twisted. All she wanted to do was to go to bed, to collapse into a dreamless sleep and wake up in a newer, better world. A world where Alex was still alive, where there were no children in the forest, women in the water, or shadows above them all. Maybe a world where Dr. Ambert was still alive.

"I should have gotten Andrea out of the city." Her father spoke now. His voice was haggard, rough. "She and Edward raised me, after they took me from my father."

It was the saddest smile Torie had ever seen on his face, and he turned it towards Edward.

"Your uncle, Edward. He was so different from you. You love to read. You're so smart for your age. Edward learned to read, but not much else. But he was smart in other ways. He could read people, he could make a plan…when he left my father, he had every intention of coming back for me. Being a cop was the only way to make money fast back then. I don't think he liked the corruption in the Margería police, though I never asked him about it. But he made his money fast. It wasn't much, not after he took me in with Andrea. Hell, I'm only five years older than my nephew.

"I should have gotten them out of there." His voice broke now. "I owed my brother that much. I could have saved his family."

"No, William." Mother sat beside him now. They were on the

floor, slouched over each other. The light from outside the windows was receding behind the trees. The afternoon was slowly going dark.

"He was my whole reason for getting into politics." Father's voice was now almost a sad, dim whisper. "I wanted to make a country where no one would have to work so hard as he did. He worked so hard, and it *killed* him. Edward, you never got to know the man you were named after, because he was too good for this world. And Christopher," Father now turned towards them, "they killed the man *you* were named after because *he* was too good for this world too!"

"Patriots," a new voice spoke out from the radio. "Antiochans, the army leadership has betrayed the nation."

Father stood up now and walked to the radio, as if convinced that coming closer would allow him to see better.

"General Kristoff and the army high command have betrayed the nation. They have sought to implicate President Ambert in a supposed Marxist plot. But it is *they* who are connected to the rebels, and who mean to surrender the country to them."

"What the hell is happening out there?" Father asked aloud. Was he aware that he was swaying on his feet? Did he know his voice was shaking?

"The true sons of Antioch, *your* sons, are retaking the country for you. We have seized this station. We will seize the others. Hold fast to each other and be together, as our country always has."

"William," Mother ventured. "You know General Kristoff."

"I do. He doesn't have a Marxist bone in his body. In fact…I've never met anyone more disinterested in politics. I…can't believe he would coup, let alone on behalf of some leftist insurgency."

"Then who's fighting him? Who's taking the stations from the army?"

"I don't know."

For a long time, the room was silent. The time for dinner passed, then bed. Father turned on the gas lamps, and the whole family crouched in the orange light and waited for the radio to speak again.

When it finally did, the whole world outside the windows was black.

***

July 16, 19__, 3 am. Broadcast from "National Radio"

My fellow countrymen, my name is Colonel Jaime Gardner, and it is with heartbreak that I speak with you today.

President Ambert is dead.

Tonight, Margería bled.

Troops under the direct command of Army Chief General Kristoff stormed the capital in the early afternoon, taking the legislature and the Supreme Court by force. For four hours, these traitors executed state officials for the sake of seizing power for themselves. While we do not have a full count yet, we estimate that at least twenty-five senators and congressmen are dead.

All nine justices, regrettably, could not be saved.

For his part, President Ambert died in the presidential residence, by all accounts heroically. He is not survived by his wife, nor by any of his three children.

In the wake of this unutterable savagery, President Ambert must instead be survived by all of us. Our mothers, fathers, and children.

Brothers and sisters, I speak to you today having seen the new horrors which await our country, but also having seen the unbreakable will of our people.

Under my command, Antioch's true sons have retaken the capital. General Kristoff has been captured, and any soldier who betrayed

their country is urged to surrender immediately or face quick repri-
sal. I have seen the bravery and endurance of our people, brothers
and sisters, but we will endure traitors no more.

I speak to you not only out of sadness, but out of anger and justice.

I issue to you a proclamation of hope, the promise of a better fu-
ture if we work together as countrymen.

For too long, Antioch has suffered. She has suffered from traitors,
from those who would mean to subdue her by force. But they will
learn, just as so many others have before them, that Antioch will
not be subdued.

I issue to you a call to arms. The armed forces, the true sons of
Antioch, are on our way to help you.

In the hard work ahead, you are not alone.

I am with you. And I will never leave you.

Protect your loved ones, hold your children tight.

We will transform our nation together.

For the glory of Antioch.

INFILTRÁTION

William sometimes regretted that he hadn't continued on with
the army and advanced past the rank of captain. But he was
young when he left, and had no knack for war or soldiery. He'd
retained a respect for professional officers, though, who began
to treat him as something of an equal when he was first elected
to public office. In his role as senator, and particularly a senator
from a political party the armed forces were traditionally skeptical of, he worked to understand the Antiochan military's needs
and concerns so as to express them better to his fellows. In all
his meetings, formal and informal, with General Kristoff, he'd
never had the impression of a man who would betray his nation.

But he *had* heard of Colonel Gardner.

Officers, no matter their rank, always seemed to change when his name was spoken. Their tone changed, as if they were discussing not a subordinate officer, but a monster. A phantom or urban legend. Their voices would go quiet. Their eyes would drift far away. William had never met the colonel, but General Kristoff himself had once said, "They actually say he has supernatural powers. That's there's a 'devil in the barracks.'" At the time, the general had merely scoffed.

General Kristoff had been tired then. An old warrior. Did he know his days were numbered? Did he know what was coming next, even then?

In some senses, William thought it would have been easier had General Kristoff betrayed Antioch. Kristoff would have allowed William to take his family and leave the country. They were friends. This Gardner, though.

Perhaps María Martin knew him. She was close with the army too, in fact much closer than William himself. Surely she had met the young officer. Maybe she could negotiate a way out for them.

Better still, maybe she would tell him that there was nothing to fear in Gardner. That the young officer was loyal to democracy, and would return the country to its elected leaders in a year's time.

Around him, the children were asleep. They did not look quiet or comfortable. Shadows had already formed under their eyes, and Torie seemed to twitch nervously beneath the blanket he and Emelda had draped over her.

Téa slept still in Emelda's lap, leaning against her mother. Emelda's eyes were dry, but also wide open.

What could they say to each other?

They were both afraid to leave the room, too afraid to leave their family, to go somewhere where they were unable to see any of their children, lest they disappear.

"You were right," Emelda said softly.

William looked at her, confused.

"You were right; they need to learn to shoot. I hate it. But they need to learn."

"Things will be okay, Emelda." He said it because it needed to be true. He needed to make it true.

Emelda shook her head. "Things already aren't okay, William. I don't know who Gardner is, but do you really think he's going to distinguish between the president and his friends? Do you really think people are going to forgive the Socialist Party for being even loosely associated with the Holy Swords?"

"I—"

"No, William. You're a good man, and you try so hard to see the good in everyone else. But I'm telling you right now, we need to be careful. If this Gardner finds us, there's no telling what sort of man we're facing."

"I'll talk to María tomorrow, Emelda. She'll probably know who he is."

"I yelled at her today, William. I said horrible things to her."

"María is…many things. But she's not one to hold a grudge."

"I hope not."

Far away, there was a knock at the door. It echoed inside Casa Verde, all through its empty rooms and cavernous halls. William closed his eyes, wanted to imagine it away. But the knock sounded again.

He stood up, careful to show Emelda the pistol he had at his side.

"You need to wake the children up. Hide them somewhere in the house."

"William—"

"Please, Emelda."

He left the room as Emelda was gently waking Christopher up. As he walked away, he heard her gently explaining what was happening.

Casa Verde seemed more haunted now than ever before. From nearly every wall, Thomas Holcomb looked down and smiled. How would he have responded to the fall of his nation? What would he have made of this young colonel and his takeover? Neither Holcomb nor the black dog at his feet offered any answers.

The knocking continued, gently.

"Senator Esquival."

William recognized Antonio's voice. He opened the doors wide.

Antonio had his own tears, thin things that streamed down from his eyes and cut his cheeks in two.

"Antonio. Please, come in. Please. How are things in town?"

"Senator…"Antonio stepped through the threshold. His deep voice was hoarse now. "When we first met you told me that the president was a friend of yours. Whatever grievances I had with the man, he always seemed good and decent. I am sorry for your loss."

"I…I'm sorry too, Antonio. Please. Emelda," William called out. "It's Antonio. Ask Christopher to stay up with the children."

"Your family made it home. I am glad." Antonio smiled. "I looked for them frantically when I heard the news. But one of my fellow coachmen told me that before I could find them, Christopher had taken his mother home. He was quite impressed by the young man's handling of the crisis."

"We are too."

They returned to the living room. Thus far, the radio had

made no new announcements, but it would be better to be close in case one should arise.

"Antonio, what about your family? Your wife?"

"As resilient a woman as this nation has ever made. A true pillar of my life, that one."

Emelda came into the room with a glass of water. She handed it to Antonio, who took it with a half-hearted smirk. "Thank you, Madame Esquival."

"Please, Antonio, just call me Emelda."

"No, madame. This nation has changed overnight. Is *still* changing. But the day I lose my manners is the day I lose myself. And simply...I cannot have that."

"Antonio." William tried to steer the conversation back. "How are things in town?"

At the question, Antonio's face turned grave. The tired smile left him.

"Senator, you have lost one friend...but I am afraid you have lost another."

"What do you mean?"

Antonio took William's hands in his own. It was the most informal, most intimate gesture the groundskeeper had given him since they'd first met last week—a week that now seemed a lifetime ago.

"Senator Martin has been killed. By the communists."

The Holy Swords had bashed María's face in with rocks. They kidnapped her from her home and took her into the woods. They stabbed her forty times. They carved their symbol into her back, and left her hanging outside a hotel. They left a note at her feet. A declaration that they had killed "the last of the old, fascist dinosaurs."

"They're threatening us," Antonio explained. "They want us to stand down and let them occupy the town. The note said two days. They're giving us two days to surrender."

"But no one intends on doing that?" William asked, already well aware of the answer.

Antonio smirked and shook his head. "No. Rio Rojo has been preparing for precisely this scenario for many years. The communists do not understand because they, like the rest of the country, look down on us. They do not understand how well we are armed, how well we know our forests and riverbeds."

He clenched his fists.

"They were only able to kill Senator Martin because they took us by surprise. By announcing themselves, they have given away their existence and their presence. I suspect that by tomorrow night, most of them will be dead."

"Antonio." Now Emelda spoke. "Is my family safe here?"

"Once we clear the town of the communists."

"No," Emelda corrected him. "That's not what I'm asking. How will the people here react to the presence of a socialist senator now that María Martin is dead? And Antonio, I need the truth: how are the people reacting to what happened in the capital today?"

For a moment, Antonio was silent, gathering his thoughts as best he could.

"Madame, I can promise you that the town's reverence for the Esquival family is unconditional. You are our guests. You are the occupants of Casa Verde. This has not changed."

"What happens if the army comes here, Antonio?" William had always admired his wife's straightforwardness, her ability in times of crisis to make it seem as if she was made of steel. "Are you going to accept the military government, if it arrives here?"

"The army is only 5,000 strong right now. They will go where the communists are. If we kill them all here, they will not come."

"And if they do?" Emelda pressed.

"Then…then I truly do not know. That is my honest answer."
Antonio took another drink of water and sighed. "The people of
Rio Rojo have felt abused by the citizens of the capital for decades
now, since the Founder's death, truly. I cannot imagine that they
would accept any government unless it could prove itself."

"Are they stupid?"

"Emelda!" William attempted to stop his wife.

"No, no. I need you both to understand this now." Emelda
was growling. "If I believed that it would protect my children, I
would sell my immortal soul. I will not let my children die because Rio Rojo wants to suddenly assert its independence. Better that I can live above the dirt with them than lie beneath it."

"I understand, Madame Esquival. But…but I have come to
ask something of your husband."

She didn't take her eyes off him. Evidently, it affected Antonio, who hesitated before speaking.

"Senator Esquival, I understand that you yourself were a soldier once?"

"Yes."

"Would you consider accompanying some of our militia tomorrow?"

"No," Emelda answered.

"Emelda—"

"No, goddamn it!" She struck her fist against the table. "If
we're in danger, William, I need you with me. I don't want to do
this on my own!"

"You're not—"

"Madame Esquival"—Antonio spoke as a man defeated—"I
understand what you must be going through. But *you* must understand: I only ask your husband to come with us to the woods
because the work in the forest will be far less gruesome than the
work that will be done in the town."

William finally understood. His stomach fell. His face went cold. He turned to Emelda, who caught his look of dark epiphany. The anger left her face.

"What's going to happen in town tomorrow, Antonio?"

"Tomorrow? Senator, it's already started."

The three adults sat quietly.

In the silence, they could faintly make out the sounds of gunshots and screaming.

***

In the dark, it was easy enough for Christopher to imagine what was happening in Rio Rojo. He didn't take his brother and sisters far: only to the closest bedroom, a former servant's room with a twin bed. They were stayed on the first floor, close enough to hear every word between Antonio and their parents.

But eventually he grew frustrated with himself. He wasn't protecting them. What good would his eavesdropping do them? How would they feel safer, knowing that Senator Martin was dead?

"Come on," he said.

Edward and Torie looked at him, puzzled. Téa was asleep, slouched against him. He remembered when Edward once leaned against him, when they were very young.

"Don't you want to know what they're saying, Christopher?" Edward asked.

Something was wrong with Edward. He was tired, but there was something else there. Something beyond simple fear.

"So much has happened today. I just want to sleep," Christopher said.

It was the truth. He was wide awake, but all he wanted to do was to close his eyes.

He didn't need to imagine what was going on in Rio Rojo, didn't need to picture the death squads patrolling the streets. His blood ran cold at the thought of men and women being dragged out of their homes, their hotel rooms, and shot. It ran even colder imagining Alma Sales holding a rifle to someone's head.

But the shots rang out every minute. Far too frequent for the violence below to be anything other than a massacre.

"Will you be able to sleep…in all of this?" Edward asked.

"Probably not," Christopher told his little brother. "But I'll have to, eventually. So will you."

"I—I—" Edward never stuttered.

Christopher realized that he had never once seen his little brother cry. But there he was, collapsed on his knees, tucked into himself and rocking back and forth. Edward had never cried in front of him.

Torie rushed to her brother, rubbing his back and telling him to hush. But he swatted her away and shook his head.

"I'm supposed to be *strong*. But I wasn't strong. Torie needed me to be strong, but I wasn't! It's easier for everyone if I'm okay. But—but I'm *not* okay!"

The last words were a high-pitched squeak. Christopher heard his brother struggling to breathe, wheezing and coughing.

Téa stirred lightly in his arms. Christopher motioned to Torie, asking her to take her sister. Torie took her gently, and Téa never woke up.

Christopher sat down beside his brother. "You've got nothing to be sorry about. You know, someone pointed out today that I haven't been a good big brother. Maybe not for a long time."

Edward's breathing steadied. It still shook, like a bird furiously caught in his throat.

"It's not okay. That I pushed you away for as long as I did. And I'm sorry. But…maybe it's okay not to be strong all the time,

Eddie. Maybe we can take turns being strong for each other?"

Christopher gently turned his brother to him. Edward lashed his arms around his back and wailed into his shoulder.

For a long time, it was enough to drown out the gunfire below.

***

When Edward finally fell asleep, Torie helped Christopher walk up the stairs. She carried Téa, and Christopher carried Edward.

Torie had forgotten how handsome her oldest brother was. She remembered teasing him once, when he was on his way to school, running around him and announcing that he would come home married. Christopher had only been ten years old then, but she already thought the world of him.

But he got so mean, so bitter and distant, Torie sometimes forgot she had a brother other than Edward.

But she saw him then, the little boy who had gotten big, holding his younger brother.

"Thank you, Christopher," she said.

They walked to her bedroom and placed Téa and Edward on the same bed. As if out of an instinctual need for comfort, they rolled towards each other.

"What happened, Torie?"

She didn't hesitate in telling. About the children in the woods. The shadow between the trees. About the woman in the water who wouldn't bleed, and who'd tried to drag Edward into the water with her. Not once did Christopher's face change; not once did it seem like he didn't believe her.

When she finished, she sighed.

"I know you don't believe me, and that's okay. You don't have to believe me. But it doesn't make it any less real."

"I believe you, Torie."

"What!? Why?"

He pointed to the window outside. Torie walked over.

The children no longer waited in the woods. She could see them below, like so many ghastly fireflies. Some walked slowly; others ran furiously on all fours. If Mother and Father would only look outside, they would see them!

But they were more afraid of the voices on the radio, of the gunshots in the air, than any ghosts or shadows.

"You're very brave, Torie."

Was this what bravery felt like? Because she felt empty. Tired. It wasn't that the fear had left her, but that it had become so big and so constant that it now seemed irrelevant. Torie just forgot she was afraid, the same way she forgot she was breathing.

"I think...if I had seen those things earlier, before today," Christopher said, "I would have screamed."

She *had* screamed. But Mother hadn't believed her. Because Torie was always scared, and always screaming. So when it mattered most, it hadn't mattered at all.

"Christopher. Have you ever loved someone?"

Her brother didn't answer for a long time. Torie didn't look back towards him, but kept her eyes on the children.

"I don't know...maybe."

"I loved a boy. He's dead now. I spent all last night crying. I'm so tired. But it won't stop."

Now she looked back. Even in the dark, the expression on her brother's face was clear. His own exhaustion, his own hurt just beneath a smile.

"Can I lean on you?" she asked.

"Sure," Christopher said.

She sat on the bed next to her brother and leaned against him. There was a comfort in a heartbeat, gentler than a pillow. "Will you scratch my head? Like Father used to?"

"Of course."

She closed her eyes. Outside the gunshots still burst, occasionally carrying screaming and crying with them. But behind her eyes it was dark, cool and calm. Inside her room, her brothers and sister were close by. Inside her home, Mother and Father stood guard.

And though she didn't truly know if she was safe, she let herself feel safe.

***

Note from the Holy Swords, found on the corpse of María Martin:

To the citizens of Rio Rojo, we bring a declaration of freedom. No longer will you suffer under the neglect of a capital that despises you, or a capitalist class that exploits you. Thomas Holcomb brought revolution to Antioch through Rio Rojo, and now we bring revolution to you in his legacy.

Tonight, the last of the fascist dinosaurs dies. And for you, we will make quick work of their children. We urge you to join us, to cast off your chains and walk as free people. To unburden yourself from the yoke of this nation's dying politics and breathe free and unhindered. Unexploited and unconquered.

Those who assist us will join Holcomb as this nation's heroes. As its liberators and heroes. Those who stand against us will suffer the same fate as all other enemies of our country, internal or external. We urge you to consider the future, to imagine your lives two days from now.

Long live Antioch.

Long may its revolution reign.

CARNIVAL

In the morning, Emelda felt as though she had been drinking. She woke up with a headache and a rolling in her stomach. She was confused to be sleeping on the couch, to squint and see William slouched in a chair across from her, his face against the armrest and rifle slung across his lap.

She wondered if it had been a dream, but only for a moment.

"Citizens," Gardner's voice came through on the radio again.

He read off the names of the dead legislators recovered in the army's retaking of the capital. There were too many names for her, too many people she personally knew. Too many faces. She was sick, painfully so. She wanted to take her family somewhere far away, to watch the horror unfold from some foreign capital where she would only have to be sad, not scared.

She roused herself slowly, throat dry and stomach empty. She would need to eat something; they all would. Even as the world was collapsing, they would still need to eat.

Antonio had described the situation to them the night before. The town had discovered that the Holy Swords had already sent sympathizers, partisans to Rio Rojo, some years in advance. Antonio knew this because one of María Martin's kidnappers had been captured shortly after they hung her body. He had been fast, but not faster than a horse. And, after a mile being drug behind that horse, the boy had told them everything he knew.

The story made her nauseous. Emelda was no stranger to blood or the injuries of war. She had treated her share of deep cuts, broken bones, infections and more. But without seeing it for herself, the images of María's tattered, lacerated body and this unknown young man being dragged through the gravel seemed more horrible than any rotting limb.

William stirred across from her when she began to walk towards the kitchen. For just a second he seemed normal, a tired man rising from an uneven, incomplete sleep. Then the memories set into his face. And with them, the misery.

"Are you hungry?" she asked.

He shook his head.

"Me either, but we need to eat. The kids need to eat too."

The mention of the children brought something to his expression. Not happiness, but maybe a sense of purpose. "Do you want me to help you cook?" he asked, still groggy.

"If you'd like."

The monotony, the mundaneness of preparing breakfast was enough for her. With William in the kitchen, cracking eggs and whisking them in a bowl, thin yellow morning-light covering him in gold, it seemed normal. Peaceful. There was an escape in not thinking about anything other than slicing avocados. In preparing rice. She could see it in his face too, how the enormity of the night before seemed to lift itself off of him with every sunny second in the kitchen.

"I remember when I fell in love with you," William abruptly said. "We were taking a cab back from a restaurant. I know we dated for a long time before I told you I loved you, and while I always thought you were beautiful, I never knew I was in love with you. But on that night, you told a joke, and you made yourself laugh. And here I was, caught off guard by whatever you had said, so stunned not only that you said it, but that you were laughing at yourself, that I didn't say anything. But then... I felt this peace. This calm."

He laughed. "I feel that way now."

Emelda stopped and looked at her husband. He was tired, but he was still strong. The lines on his face were there, echoes of a sad life. But the smile on his face was wide.

"You never told me that," she said.

He grinned now, wickedly. "You want to know the funniest part of that story, though?"

"What?"

"I can't remember the joke."

She snorted, and wild, uncontrollable laughter escaped her. It proved infectious, as soon William was laughing even louder than she was. They leaned on each other, sighing and coughing until they could be quiet again.

"Do you know when I fell in love with you?" she asked.

"No, but every day I'm thankful."

"Our first conversation," she said, with a little bit of sadness, "Is that bad? That I loved you first?"

He squeezed her to him. "I'm just glad you did. I'm sorry that I took so long to catch up to you."

"I'm just glad you did, too."

***

William's first task was to search the remnants of the communists' homes.

Antonio explained that the people of Rio Rojo had anticipated that the Holy Swords were living among them, long before the Esquivals ever arrived. There had been a long project of slow surveillance, of scratching hammers and sickles into the side walls of homes, suspected secret meeting places. Any successful insurgency would need to take a riverport, and as the symbolic birthplace of the nation, of Holcomb's home, Rio Rojo would be a symbolic conquest too.

But now, in the daylight that followed a long, horrible night, Rio Rojo only seemed a wreck of itself: a pale, parched skeleton of shattered windows, broken doors and streaks of bloody dirt.

The first corpse he saw was that of a young man, rolled over on his back along the side of the road. The blood around his stomach had already gone brown and black, his hands still buried in his own gore as if he could stop his life from slipping out between his fingers. Another corpse followed behind a horse, a rope still around its red ragdoll face.

But there were more tucked away, in living rooms and closets. The people of Rio Rojo took no chances with strangers, and the hammer and sickle, discreetly carved on a wall or post, was a death sentence enough.

With Antonio, he moved slowly through the now-empty homes.

The evidence of the executions was all around them. In the scattered papers. The overturned furniture. The red blossoms of human remains streaked across floors and walls.

They opened all the drawers, the closets and overturned the beds.

In five houses they found proof. Pamphlets from the Holy Swords, hand-drawn diagrams of the town. Newspaper clippings. Books by María Martin, certain passages underlined.

More often than not, though, they only found photos. A young girl in a simple dress. An old man smiling over a piece of cake. Grim reminders that the condemned, guilty and innocent, were whole lives and universes snuffed out in a moment of thunder and gore.

William and Antonio kept silent. What could be said between them? Who could hold onto their hate in the quiet after death? William reflected that there was an instinct to reconcile at funerals, to abandon grudges for the sake of the dead who could no longer enjoy the peace. But there was no peace coming soon.

In the silence of the broken, hollowed town, William could still hear gunshots from the woods. Still smell small fires burning in the alleys. Whatever quiet or peace that existed before was only temporary.

Moving through the ruined homes, William felt more terror than he ever had before. More than in the home of Ulysses
Esquival, whose outbursts of violence could begin and end at
any moment. More than he had when his company had broken
through into Calgría, where he knew his death would be final
but quick. A terror made greater because he knew that his wife
and children were waiting for him on the hill. A terror made
greater because he knew that he would have to try and tell them
what he saw happening just outside their home.

He heard a crying in the street.

People were making gallows from the balconies of their homes
and shops. Men, and a few women, hung under slowly twisting
ropes.

William looked up at one man, still standing. There was a gun
pointed at his ribs. He was an old man, with grey hair and messy
beard. A man whose name he did not know but whose face he
recognized from the period of anguish that preceded Emelda's
waited arrival to the town. A man who smiled at him, and called
him "Señor Esquival."

The man had looked at William with such honesty then. And
now, the contorted, pink-faced anguish in his face seemed honest too.

"Puh-please," he spoke. "I only did what you asked. Take me
to the woods. Bury me there! Don't let me hang where my family can see me. Please! "

But his executioner hoisted him off of his feet and threw him
from the balcony.

The rope snapped with his neck. The man was heavy, and
the fall was short. He wallowed on the ground, moaning from
beneath white-pink spit.

William moved forward, to get a closer look.

Every creature deserved mercy. Nothing should be made to suffer.

The old man seemed to recognize him, because a light came to his eyes when he met William's.

"I only did what they wanted."

But the man's face was no longer there.

His lips, teeth and tongue were gone.

Smoke wafted up from the barrel of Antonio's rifle.

And somewhere else, another man wept.

***

Christopher understood that their breakfast needed to be normal.

The faces at the table were still tired, still haggard and marked red with tears. But they were given to temporary lapses of smiling, of spontaneous and inexplicable laughter. His mother even hummed while she served herself eggs.

So he didn't mention the ghosts.

Not yet.

He would tell their parents; he'd promised Torie. He would tell them that *he* saw them, that they weren't imaginary and they weren't *normal*. He wasn't sure they would believe him, or if that would even matter. Christopher knew better by now, that there was no reason to be more afraid of monsters than people. It didn't matter that the children in the forest glowed, or that they had no eyes. Death squads were also in the forest, and there were more reason to be scared of guns than ghosts.

So it wouldn't matter if ghosts were real, or if his parents believed him. They were trapped. There was nowhere to stay but in their haunted home.

But after his promise, Torie had been relieved enough to fall asleep. After his promise, Edward had thanked him. Now at the table, his siblings even seemed calm. Every now and then, they would turn to him and he would offer a weak, tired smile. They grinned back, and it made Christopher's heart beat a little softer. Téa sang over her eggs, angelically oblivious.

If there was any God, any mercy for his family, Christopher decided that it was that at least one of them was young enough to not understand what was happening. That maybe there was someone who would live through this and say, "Oh, I don't really remember, I was so young then." Someone who would, maybe, only remember a big empty house with paintings of the same towering, stoic man throughout.

Christopher told his little brother that it was okay. That it was his turn to be the strong one, to be stronger so they could rest. But Mother was smiling, and everyone looked happy.

He would be stronger a little longer, and then he would tell her.

Before he left, his father handed him a rifle.

"There's a box of bullets in our room. If something happens, take everyone and hide. Just hide."

As William turned away, Christopher told him, "There are ghosts in the woods."

Christopher wasn't sure what he expected, what he needed from his father in that moment. But Father merely looked confused. For a second his mouth opened, as if he were going to ask something else. But Antonio called after him, and William merely said, "We'll talk when I get home."

It had been enough to keep him quiet, enough to make himself silent and let his mother pretend she was happy. He watched her now.

Father had left her a pistol, which was on the coffee table next to the couch where she lay sleeping with Téa in her arms. With her eyes closed, Mother seemed healthier, like the life was coming back to her. What sense was there in waking her? How could it do anything but make things worse?

There was a knock at the door.

Christopher held the rifle in his hands and walked slowly through the halls. Thomas Holcomb's green eyes looked down on him as he moved, careful not to tremble or shake.

He approached the main entryway, and crouched.

"Christopher," a soft voice spoke from beyond the door. "Are you there?"

Alma!

He ran to the door and opened it wide.

Whatever had happened during the night had left no mark on her. She seemed well rested, even in good spirits. There was color in her cheeks. A kindness in her eyes.

"Are you okay?" she asked. "How is your family? Your mother?"

"They're fine. Alma…what are you doing here?"

When she smiled, he could see her teeth, clean and white.

"The Youth Rifle Brigade has been taking patrol in the woods. I also wanted to keep you safe. So I've been patrolling the woods around Casa Verde all night."

"You—" He stopped. He looked behind him. Casa Verde seemed empty now. Quiet, with Mother and Téa asleep, Torie and Edward upstairs. He stepped out and shut the door as quietly as he could. "You were patrolling outside our house last night?"

"Yes."

"Did you see them?"

"The insurgents? Not until—"

"No, not the insurgents. The *ghosts*."

Her smile faded. The gunshots were more infrequent now, but in the long quiet Christopher could hear them. The world seemed calm, but pregnant with dread, the blue sky and vibrant green forest only a witness to something awful.

"*Ghosts*," she said. Her voice was low now.

"Yes," Christopher whispered back quickly. "Glowing children."

Alma was still. Would she answer him? Would she say anything at all, or was she going to walk away? He could see in her face that she believed him. But instead of fear or even sympathy, there was an indignation. As if he had seen or said something he shouldn't have.

"They're only *children*, Christopher. They can't help themselves."

It was like the air had been sucked out of him.

"This whole country is built on a graveyard. But there are more bodies under Rio Rojo…and time has taken everything from them. It's only natural that they're wild. You shouldn't hold it against them."

"I…what do you mean?"

"We don't call them 'ghosts' here. Calling them 'ghosts' means that they're not people. We've already taken their names. They should be able to keep their humanity."

"What…do you call them?"

"What they are. Brothers. Sisters. Sons and daughters."

"They're scaring *my* brother and sisters. They're watching them at night."

"It's only natural, Christopher. They're scared of the forest. It's only natural they want to come inside."

His head was reeling. Whatever reaction, revelation, he had expected, this wasn't it.

"I'll show you." She smiled, and the warmth came back to her voice. "I came here to show you something, anyway. A bit of good news."

"But I—"

"Your family is safe. We have riflemen all around the perimeter. And you'll be safe with me. I'll protect you."

She held out a hand, and he was caught off guard again. How lovely it was.

He held her hand in his own, and followed her into the forest.

***

By noon, William had seen more corpses in a day than he had in an entire war.

The people of Rio Rojo were still dragging their condemned neighbors from their homes and hotel rooms, their fingers bleeding as they gripped onto splinters. He was beginning to understand what this was. What began as retribution, revenge, was quickly spiraling out of control. People were bringing up their old hatreds and grudges, letting them bubble to the surface like cold, black water beneath the dirt.

The dying no longer denied they were communists. Now they only screamed "Sorry."

Sorry for stealing. For cheating. For lying. Sorry for being born. For having my father's last name.

But please. Please tell me it's not worth killing me over.

You know me. You know I can't be a traitor. Not to our nation. Not to our town.

So brother. Sister. Please tell me. Please tell me you forgive me.

Please.

But if there was any forgiveness to be offered, it was not in this life. Not in these long hours.

Still, William kept quiet atop his horse, well aware that at any moment the waters could change, that he himself might have to wade into the violence. To prove his loyalty. To protect his family.

He forgot to drink water. Forgot that the sun was still hanging, still shining above them despite the horror beneath it. The world was eating itself alive, and the sky wouldn't even grant the mercy of darkness. Too much to witness. Too much for any man to see.

William lost track of the time. The screams. The needs of his body.

The world entered a haze of red and sky blue. A whirlwind of begging and bleeding.

The stench of slaughter.

The squelching of too-wet dirt beneath horse hooves.

And then the world began to shift. To spin.

He leaned from his horse. Bile, hot and sour, forced itself up from his stomach.

"Please, Senator!" Antonio pleaded. He offered William a canteen of water.

In a daze, William took it to his lips. It was hot, and hit his stomach painfully. He winced.

"Please. Let us go, let us sit in the shade for just a moment."

Would there be any arguing? Was there anything to say at all? Would it be better to simply follow orders? Suggestions? There would be a tomorrow after this, and a tomorrow after that. He could reach them; he knew he could.

He followed Antonio and his horse, letting the coachmen guide them away from the town, through neighborhood after dying neighborhood. More than once the smell of shit and blood almost made him fall.

What was this?

William found himself towards the edge of the forest, beneath the canopy of the trees. The grass was soft beneath him, and Antonio smiled gently. There was bread in his hands, and it was sweet in his mouth.

"You must have never witnessed anything like this, Senator."

"I saw combat," William affirmed. "When...I killed a man, I knew he had been armed. That he was a man just like me. Ready to kill, just like me. But..." He looked at Antonio. "But I don't know what this is."

"It's a sacrifice, Señor."

"A *sacrifice?*"

"The army...they will enter Rio Rojo if they do not understand that we are ready."

"So this is all to scare them away? Antonio—" The bread settled his stomach. The water cooled his mind. His thoughts, composure returned to him.

"Do you know that they *despise* Rio Rojo in the barracks? Do you know that we called Rio Rojo *unpatriotic*, because they sent so few of their children to join our ranks?"

"I—"

"Don't try to justify this." William realized with horror that the words were crawling out of him, that his righteous indignation had forced its way out of him. He felt the same passion, the same valor as when he confronted bankers, the wealthy, the criminally greedy.

"If not a sacrifice...then an offering."

"*What?*"

"An *offering.*"

That was enough. This was absurd. *Evil.* "I need to be with my family."

"Senator! We need you *here.*"

"For what?" William laughed. "Do you want me to lie? To tell the army that the people of Rio Rojo did what was necessary? What was right? That you are all patriots? I don't know what kind of man Colonel Gardner is, but I'll tell him all the lies I need to keep my family alive."

William turned towards his horse.

"Senator."

William met Antonio's eyes, then saw the barrel of his rifle.

***

Christopher followed Alma through the woods carefully.

She knew every branch and root in the jungle, and made sure to show Christopher where any obstacle might be. He concentrated on her intently, worried that if he looked away from her back, he would see another glowing face peeking from behind a bush.

She'd said there was nothing to be afraid of, but he was. Not of dying, but of something he couldn't explain. He could explain the coup, the communists. But the children in the forest. They might not kill him, or even hurt him, but that wasn't enough to make him any less afraid.

"You want to know about them? The brothers and sisters?"

He didn't offer a reply.

"They did what they needed to do for the country."

"What they needed to do?"

"Die," she said, as if it was the simplest thing, the most obvious thing. "They died."

"I don't understand, Alma."

"There are more things you can do for a nation than *fight* for it. Thomas Holcomb, your great ancestor, fought for this nation. Fought the British, then his own countrymen, to unify it. But he was not the only founder." She looked back at him, her blue eyes bearing into him. "So many people gave their lives for this country. So many of them *hurt* for this country. But they don't hurt anymore."

"I—"

"It's no easy thing, to sacrifice. But these are uneasy times."

Ahead of them Christopher could see a clearing. They moved in slowly. He blinked furiously, letting the tears water his eyes so he could see again.

Michael and Andre Pervin stood by a tree. Between them, tied against it, was the waiter from the café.

"I'd been tracking Sampson for months."

Alma was smiling wildly now, the same way she had smiled at him the day before, when he'd realized she was drawing faces to shoot at.

Sampson was bloodied and his face was bruised. There was a white rag in his mouth, but it was pink and red with spittle. For a moment, Christopher hoped he was unconscious. But then Andre Pervin punched him in the stomach.

The man screamed from the bottom of his throat. Muffled though it was, Christopher thought it was the loudest thing he had ever heard.

Andre hit him again. "Fucking commie scum!"

Sampson cried and wept. An animal, understanding it was hurt but not understanding why.

"Sampson was sent by the Holy Swords central command. He's a spy. They thought that since his father was from Rio Rojo, we would trust him when he came home."

Alma looked like a wolf. Her eyes were burning. Her teeth were sharp.

"But being from a place is different from being loyal to it."

She walked forward, towards Sampson and the Pervin brothers.

Alma stopped in front of them, scooping a bit of dirt in her hands. She slid down the rag in Sampson's mouth and shoved the dirt in.

Before he could scream, before he could cough it out, the gag was back on. Sampson coughed furiously, dirt seeping out from the sides of his mouth.

"You killed María Martin, Sampson. Maybe you never put a knife in her, but you invited in the people who did. You were going to kill the Esquival family next. But we found your comrades. And we found you."

She turned to Christopher. "He found you too."

Christopher understood.

His chest hurt. It *burned*. There was a pounding in his head, a scream in the back of his mind. He shook, oh *God*, he shook!

Alma's wolf smile left, replaced with something gentler. She walked to him, back to his side. She placed his rifle in his hands. She lifted his arms.

"I understand," she whispered in his ear.

Sampson was howling now.

In the dark behind the trees, the children were looking on.

Every part of him was cold. His arms. His fingers.

Alma's hand wrapped around his. She spread his shoulders. His feet.

She leaned him against her. His finger, their fingers against the trigger.

"I'll teach you," she whispered. "It's okay."

Christopher didn't feel the rifle kick back against him. Didn't hear the bullet leave the gun.

There was something ruined above Sampson's neck.

In the dark, a glowing white face was streaked with red.

***

William walked with his hands behind his head.

Antonio held the rifle steady, as William saw when he looked back only once. The sounds of the slaughter in the town faded away. The cicadas and hummingbirds fluttered around them, covering the sound of wet dirt and leaves beneath their feet. Faintly, though only faintly, strings of sunlight poured a little grey into an otherwise green world.

"How far are we going, Antonio?"

"Not much farther now, Senator."

William laughed. "Honestly…if you mean to kill me, there's no more need for honorifics."

"You're wrong. A man is nothing if not his manners."

"Were you kind when you killed those people in the town? Did you call them 'señor' or 'señora?'"

"We're doing what we have to here!"

"You're not the first person to say that. You won't be the last."

"No, you're wrong! If all goes well, if all goes according to her plan, no child in Antioch will go hungry again."

"'According to *her* plan.' So this was María's idea? Before she died? We've been walking in these woods for a long time, Antonio. Woods where you told me there were insurgents. And yet you have a gun on *my* back."

William kept him talking. It was a skill in politics, to draw words from mouths like water from a well. He was no stranger to long debates on the Senate floor, nor to marching to his death. There had been guns to his back before. He scanned the ground slowly.

Antonio had never served in the army, or even in the police. He might be a good shot, a sportsman or a hunter. But if William was going to keep living, if he was going to stay with his family, he needed Antonio to be a terrible fighter.

It was going to take a lot to take the gun from him. William would need to overpower him. Shock him. Surprise him. It was going to take even more to get Antonio to answer his questions.

"What are you going to do with my family? What's going to happen to them when I die?"

"There is a special plan for your family."

"Are you going to tell me that plan?"

"No."

"Why?"

"Because...Senator, you must believe that I truly do respect you. In time, I could have even come to love you as a brother. And it is out of this love that I will not tell you. I do not want your final moments to be ones of suffering.

"You will be with them again. I imagine, in a calmer place. Perhaps you might find comfort in that?"

William joined the army so that he could send checks home to his brother. Edward had married young, fathered a boy of his own. It was only right that William repay him. And as a soldier, there were plenty of opportunities to get money. Sometimes the officers would ask for special favors. Cleaning and food. Other times they would ask for more unsavory favors.

In one camp in Calgría, there had been a small building called "the shed." A one-room stone house, with dirt floors and a thatched window.

There was money to be made in the shed, if a soldier could learn how.

William saw a root up ahead, twisted up from the dirt like a gnarled arm. He picked up his pace, though not too quickly.

"Do not try to run away," Antonio said.

"Why not? What will you do, kill me?"

"No. You should die somewhere special."

"Where?" William asked.

"The river—"

Antonio stumbled.

William turned around quickly. As Antonio stumbled, his rifle bent to his left.

He bit into Antonio's left shoulder. Through the cloth he

could feel the heat bubble up, the salt and copper filling his mouth. Antonio screamed and dropped his rifle.

William spat out blood and pinned Antonio down. He stood up quickly and brought his foot down on the bleeding shoulder as hard as he could. The boot met blood and bone. Antonio screamed.

William's foot came down again. And again.

"I'm going to break your arm," William growled.

Antonio said nothing in reply. He was panting, his eyes darting out to the woods.

"I'm going to break your arm, and then I may break the other one. Then I'm going to shoot off your feet. Then your knees. But if you tell me what I want to know about this conspiracy against my family, I'll end it by putting a bullet in your head."

It was as if Antonio hadn't heard him at all. He was panicked. He needed to be reminded. Just like all those faceless bodies in the shed in Calgría.

William moved his foot from the ruined left shoulder to the right one. He bent down, grabbed Antonio's wrist, and jerked upward.

The pop was like an explosion.

Antonio wept, but William dragged him gently to lean him against a tree. There were keys to torture, something he had learned in earning money to send home. The first was time: give a man time to realize where he is. What his life is and what it will be. The second was to not forget that the thing opposite you was a man. He knew other soldiers who had worked for their bonuses by convincing themselves that the writhing things under hoods weren't people at all, but they had to chase these delusions with alcohol. With opium. Another set had reveled in their cruelty, but they killed informants too quickly to learn or earn anything useful.

William instead remembered that every man, no matter his circumstance, came to him with a life. With loves, fulfilled and unfulfilled. Pride and dignity. It was this pride, this dignity, which needed to be massaged for information. Every good soldier would be loyal. William was loyal. The only way to continue forward in torture, William knew, was carefully.

William brought a canteen to Antonio's face. Out of instinct, or maybe out of terror, Antonio took a drink.

"You need to know that I would have killed you. I would have just shot you and run home to my family, had you not told me that they were in danger. And I need you to understand that because you told me that, you and I are going to sit here for as long as it takes. And you're going to answer every one of my questions. Do you understand?"

A familiar look of defiance welled up in Antonio's dark eyes. The anger of a whipped and beaten animal. The indignation of a man realizing he must swallow his dignity.

William removed Antonio's shirt.

The wound he'd made in Antonio's shoulder was only superficial, but it had been enough to surprise him. He took the shirt and made a bundle, pressing deep into the blood.

"I'll start first," William began. "You're learning something about me that no one else knows. Not my wife. Not María Martin, rest her soul. Not anyone who voted for me. The nation asks you to do all sorts of horrible things for it, but begs your silence. Your complicity. Because if you speak, if you tell the whole and unvarnished truth, it is an indictment that goes beyond you.

"Torturing Calgrían soldiers, that crime is not just my own. It would ruin the dignity of Antioch itself. And my wife? My family? How could they look at a man who truly gave his everything, his soul, to a nation and its war effort?

"There are greater things that you can give your country than your life. And now, you know that I have."

William pressed hard into the wound.

Antonio howled.

"You earlier told me that you would have liked to love me as a brother. Then tell me a secret of your own. What is this conspiracy against my family?"

He let the question sit. Let it sink in.

Antonio wept, but quietly now. He got his breath. Around them, something rustled in the forest, but William paid it no mind. They were far from the town, but someone would come look for them eventually. And if Antonio screamed loud enough, there would be no telling who would come. William understood that. It was an acceptable risk now.

"May I," Antonio started, "begin by telling you a story about our dear Senator Martin?"

"Sure," William attempted to say, tenderly.

"It also concerns…Colonel Gardner."

William was surprised at how far his stomach seemed to fall at the mention of the colonel.

Antonio coughed up phlegm and blood. "Senator Martin was much like you…Señor. She had a special fondness for soldiers. The army loves civilians, especially politicians who love them back…a recommendation from Senator Martin for the military academy went a long way, and meeting with cadets was her opportunity to influence the development of new military leadership…new military doctrine.

"Gardner was just a cadet then…but I've never felt so *cold* as when he walked into her office. It was as if he had taken a deep breath and sucked all the oxygen, all the light, in for himself.

"Senator Martin was an expert of history. She valued other students of history. Other nationalists. So she always began her interviews with young cadets the same way." Antonio shifted himself up with his legs. It must have been painful, with both arms ruined and lost. But it was evidently important that he look William in the eye.

"'Many tried to unify Antioch before,'" he said, doing his best impression of the Senator, "'but none of them were successful until Thomas Holcomb. What made him different?'"

Antonio smiled now, as if recalling something fondly.

"Most students cite military history. The Battle of Bosque Bautismal was key in pushing the last British loyalists out of Antioch. Others explain it with Holcomb's charisma, his status as a mixed-race landowner who could unite the elite and peasant classes. But Gardner…Gardner was the only one who gave the most correct answer.

"'Thomas Holcomb made covenant with the devil.'

"We are making our own covenant, Senator Esquival, but with something greater than any devil. Gardner was wrong, but so close."

"Spell it out for me, Antonio. Make it simple."

And now Antonio did laugh. First lightly, as if bemused, and then loudly. Desperately.

"You've got Holcomb's blood, Señor. So do your children. One of you will renew Thomas Holcomb's covenant with the nation."

William's eyes slipped to the dark beneath the trees.

A young, pale face looked back. William remembered what his son had said to him this morning, what seemed like a lifetime ago now.

There are ghosts in the woods.

The face in the forest shone like a pearl, still slick from oyster slime. It had dark hair, matted and tangled with leaves and sticks. And try as he might to find its eyes, he could see nothing looking back at him.

"Ah." Antonio spoke up. He coughed up again, spit landing on his bloody shirt. "So you finally see them?"

"What am I looking at, Antonio?"

"They are *our* covenants. Made with the nation." He smiled weakly. "Little stars. Glowing forever."

"What do you mean, 'covenants'? *Antonio.*"

Somewhere close by, a shot rang out.

Antonio smiled widely. "I am sorry. I truly am. But there is a better place, for you and your family."

And he yelled.

William was quick. There was a stone at Antonio's side, a large rock that William had taken note of as soon as he began the torture. The rock was heavy enough. It came down fast on Antonio's head. There was a wet split. And then quiet.

Antonio's arms went limp and red. His ruined head slouched. The little face in the wood receded into the underbrush.

***

Téa woke up before her mother.

After the long night, the world seemed softer. There was an early morning humidity that had managed to creep into the house. Her clothes stuck to her and made her feel gross. She groaned and rubbed her eyes, finding a dull ache behind them.

Behind her, Mommy was still asleep. Tenderly, Téa got up and tried to let Mommy sleep.

She didn't think anything of this being the first time she had walked the house alone, without Torie or Edward or even Mommy. She didn't understand what was happening on the radio, what the man meant when he talked about 'sieges' and 'traitors,' but she knew everyone was sad.

Téa knew there was clean water in the refrigerator, and that there were glasses in the cupboard. She moved a chair carefully and stepped up to reach her glass. When she turned around, an eyeless child greeted her.

The little girl was only a little smaller than Téa, with a silly smile and a big, toothy grin.

Téa remembered that she'd promised Eddie she wouldn't talk to them, she'd stay away from them. But now they were out of the forest, in the house. In the daytime.

"I'm not supposed to talk to you." She turned away and went to the refrigerator.

"Why?" the little girl asked.

"You made me hurt my brother. That wasn't nice."

"We just wanted to show you something. But you're right. It wasn't nice. You can't hurt what you love. It's against the rules."

"Yes," Téa said back flatly.

"If you can't talk, can you listen?"

Téa thought carefully. "I don't think so. How'd you get into the house?"

"We've always been inside. We're free and can come and go as we please. No walls or doors can stop us. No thorns can cut us. You could be like us too. Without being afraid."

"I'm not afraid," Téa said angrily, wanting this little girl to leave her alone so she could keep her promise to her brother.

"You may think we don't have any eyes, but just because you can't see them doesn't mean they can't see you. We know you're scared. We were scared too, but we're not scared anymore. And we'll never be scared again."

And the girl told Téa about a world beneath the water. About a place where people flew and drifted slowly. A cool, calm place that was red and still. Where every minute was a song and there was no pain, hunger, or hurt. A place full of kids who were kids forever.

"All we want is to show you, show your brother this place. We only need you to come with us."

"No, I don't want to."

Behind Téa there was a gasp.

Mommy's eyes were wide. Her hands were trembling.

When she screamed, it shook the world.

***

When Edward woke up, he didn't want to get out of bed. His whole body felt heavy and useless. There was a pain just behind his eyes that wouldn't go away no matter how long he kept them closed. Hugging the pillow close to him didn't help, nor casting his blanket off so he could be cool.

He stayed in bed for one hour. And then another.

There was too much to face in the day. Too much for him to stand up. Too much for him to think about.

It was easier to close his eyes. To imagine one world while he waited for this one to end.

Edward waited for the day to go on without him, but it wouldn't.

Finally he turned over.

When had Torie lain down next to him? When had she fallen asleep?

He rose quietly.

The room hadn't changed. The world was still here. The antique furniture, the white curtains. He walked out to the window, only to find that the green gardens and dark forest still stood there.

He thought of the woman in the river. How cold her hands had been on the back of his head. How she'd smiled at him when she pulled him into the water. He thought about the red he saw, and then the black.

And he remembered, he remembered that one awful thought.

At least it's all over now.

He'd read that sometimes people saw their entire lives before they died. But Edward had just had that one thought.

Torie had pulled him out of the water.

Torie.

She must have fought off the children, must have pulled him through the woods.

He turned back to her again. When did she get so strong? So brave?

He realized he was hungry. Thirsty. And then, he couldn't focus on anything else.

He closed the door quietly behind him and walked along the second floor. He passed the library, where the portrait of Thomas Holcomb and Dragón still hung staring. What was only days ago seemed like years. The house had seemed ominous even then, but now it was honestly the thing he was afraid of the least. There were too many things out there that could kill him. Hang him. Drown him.

It did no good to be scared of faces on the wall.

He walked away from the library and towards the winding stairs, where once again Thomas Holcomb loomed over him. His great-grandfather's presence was just as oppressive, as inescapable as everything else in his life.

Mother was still asleep, sprawled across the couch as if her very soul had been flattened.

The sight rekindled something in him, a tenderness that gave him a reason to move beyond hunger and thirst.

In the kitchen, Téa was talking with a ghost.

He watched her deal with it, speak with it, as if it were a conversation with any other sort of unwelcome guest or persistent pest. Maybe it was because she was so young, she never had to be afraid of being able to tell the difference between what was real and what wasn't.

And then the ghost told her about what was under the water. The ghost told her that there wouldn't be any more hurting.

He didn't want this ghost here with them. He didn't want his little sister lured away, to drown in some river.

Behind him, Mother was swaying.

Her eyes quivered. Her mouth hung open.

The little girl with no eyes looked right back at her.

And Mother screamed. She dropped to her knees and fell. Her hands fell into her hair, and she began pulling.

"Mother!"

Edward stooped beside her.

"Mommy!"

The ghost was gone. It was only them now.

Mother was crying. Her breathing was hoarse, uneven and choking.

"Mother, please breathe. Please breathe!"

Edward rubbed his hands along her back. She was curled into herself, muttering something indistinct that Edward couldn't hear.

"Please. Please just breathe."

Téa hugged her too.

"It's too much," Mother whispered. "It's all too much."

"I know," Edward said. "I know."

"Did she see them?" Torie asked from behind them.

There was no sleep in her eyes, no fear in her face. She was resolute, asking with a tone that suggested she already knew the answer.

"Yes," Edward responded.

His mother's hand reached for his. It was so much bigger, and she squeezed it tight. But her weeping subsided to whimpering.

He remembered what Mother said the day they came up the river. That living in the devil's cradle had been a matter of survival, not choice.

He squeezed her hand back.

They would survive.

He'd make sure of it.

**

Christopher couldn't look at his hands. They weren't his hands. Not anymore.

Every step he took away from the shooting ground was wavering and difficult.

No one had told him how cartoonish it would look when he killed a man. The blood was darker than he expected, like something out of a lurid comic book. No one had told him how easy it would be to stop thinking of a corpse as a person once they stopped moving.

Alma had smiled at him, but it didn't matter. He wasn't himself anymore. It felt like something, something at the core of his being, had been ripped out of him.

Something loomed over him. A dark, hungry thing with brilliant yellow eyes. It followed him through the woods. Walked with him all the way to the doorstep of Casa Verde.

He opened the door, and it came inside.

**

Bylaws of the Rio Rojo Youth Rifle Brigade

The youth rifle brigade shall serve as a militia in the incident of an invasion

The youth rifle brigade is a patriotic, anti-communist organization

The youth rifle brigade shall train members in the use of lethal force

FLIGHT

William wandered through the forest for hours, the ghosts always trailing behind him.

He was careful to be quiet, or as quiet as he could be. Antonio had mentioned "work in the woods," and he couldn't be sure it wasn't a lie. And if there were insurgents here, if they really had killed María Martin, then they would certainly kill him as well. Massacre infected the air, and there was no longer any promise that he could trust anyone he might find to not shoot him on sight.

He needed to get back, but it would be at least a whole day's worth of walking. More, if he encountered any trouble.

His palms hurt from gripping his rifle, and his shoulders felt iron and locked.

The children watched him, but also seemed to hide from him. They would dart behind trees, dash under bushes. They never gasped or screamed, never made any sounds at all. At first he tried to approach them, to call after them. But when one turned to him, eyeless and smiling nervously, he ran away.

Christopher had called them "ghosts." Antonio, "covenants."

Whatever they were, William thanked God that they seemed as afraid of him as he was of them.

Tense but tired, he tried to pay them no mind. They had no guns to shoot him with. No horses to drag him behind. If they posed a threat, it was a lesser threat than any potential executioners patrolling the woods. The few times he heard men talking, he darted beneath the brush. But they never came close enough that he could see them, or even hear their words clearly. He would lie and wait, only thinking of Emelda and their children. Were they safe? Why hadn't he listened to her? Why had he left her alone?

The sky was beginning to darken from blue to purple. Traveling by night was going to be harder. The forest was already dark, already cutting at him with thorns and branches. His throat was dry, and the canteen at his side had been emptied hours ago. Despite his urgency to get back to his family, his knees were already stiff and his feet were already heavy.

The longer he walked, the bolder the ghosts became. They would come closer to him, crossing from the periphery of his sight and into full view. Only when he looked into the places where their eyes should have been did they back away, running away like any other shy or scared children.

He didn't know these woods, but he had a general idea of his direction. He knew he was going up the right hill. He might reach Casa Verde by midnight. And then...

And then?

He didn't know.

He would hold his family tight, and wait for the world to stop ending.

***

Like her husband, Emelda had seen her share of corpses. As a medical doctor she had seen the human form at its worst. Cut open, shriveled, ripe, discolored and ready to burst.

Over time, her zeal to make the world a better place had been replaced with a firm knowledge that there were only so many things she could do with her hands. That she only had two of them. And that no medicine in the world could save people from ruining each other, or themselves.

She hadn't regretted leaving her job, hadn't regretted watching her younger children more closely than she'd raised her first. Even with her there, she noticed Edward had grown far more independent than his brother. She enjoyed noticing the little inexplicable differences between her children, cherishing them like beautiful, pleasant secrets.

But now her children had seen a ghost.

Had it been a ghost? Or was this the term she was using because it was the only one she had? A glowing child, with swirling darkness where its eyes should be. It had smiled at her too, and when it did, she fell to the floor and wept.

In front of her children.

Now she listened to them carefully.

Edward explained that the "children" two days ago, the ones who were in the forest and supposedly stirred so much emotion in Téa that she bit her brother, were like the one they had just seen in the house. That they were cold to the touch, and that their skin wouldn't break. He told her about following Victoria into the woods, about meeting a woman in the river. A woman who cradled her to him, and tried to drag him in.

How they ran home, furiously.

And then...

Finally, she just sighed.

Her kids were good kids. In the wake of the coup, they had taken their cues from her. From William. The two of them had been so visibly afraid that the children had kept their own personal terrors to themselves.

"Here's what we're going to do," Emelda started, unsure of how she would finish. Edward and Victoria looked at her so intently, but Téa just looked confused.

"We're going to be honest with each other." She smiled. "In all my life, I've never seen something like this until today. I know what it's like, watching your parent hurt and wanting to stop it, to keep them from hurting more. I feel bad, because you kids never got to meet either of your uncles. When my brother died, it eventually killed my father. And I kept so much from him, maybe he would have lived a little longer if I hadn't. But it's my job to try and keep you kids safe as much as I can, to lie down and get between you and monsters if they come for you. Do you understand?

"But I need to be honest with you. I never believed in ghosts. Gods. Anything 'supernatural.' I was a doctor, and firmly believed that if I couldn't hold a thing in my hands, or at the very least observe it, it wasn't real. Even the stories didn't interest me. You know me, I read history. So…what should we do?"

It wasn't fair to ask them, but it was the only thing Emelda could think to do. She wanted them to start thinking logically, coldly. There may very well come a time when she wouldn't be able to protect them, or would even die for them. They would need to act the same way she did on observing a bleeding wound or a dangerous infection: carefully, slowly and precisely.

Edward and Victoria took their mother's question seriously. They buried their chins into their hands, looked up at the ceiling and frowned. It would have been cute, or maybe comical, to see her children so preoccupied in any other moment.

"Is there anywhere we can go?" Victoria asked, a little desperation in her voice.

Emelda sighed again. "There is, but you kids should understand…the whole country is going to be different for a long time. I don't know if we can get out, or at least if we can get out as easily as we could have last year."

"Leave the *country?*" Edward asked.

Emelda nodded. "Your father and I speak three languages. You kids speak two. We have a lot of options in terms of where we could go. But first we'd need to figure out how to get out of Rio Rojo, then Antioch."

"Do you think it will be hard to leave Rio Rojo?" Edward asked again.

Emelda paused as something heavy settled in her stomach. *We're going to be honest with each other.* If she had only known how hard that promise was going to be. How awful. They were already learning to shoot. To shoot to *kill.* Honesty would rob her children of their childhoods, of their smiles and their carefree laughter. After today their eyes would have a smokiness, and their smiles would be half-hearted.

"Right now…" Emelda gulped. "They're killing people in town. I imagine a lot of people. I don't think anyone is going to let us go. Even if we asked."

"Then…"

"We're going to stay put for the time being. The communists are in the woods, according to your father and Antonio, and we don't know if the army is coming or not. Honestly"—there it was again, cutting at her children and any hope they had—"the army is our best chance."

She scooped up Téa in her arms, and then took Edward and Victoria's wrists in her hands. She looked at them intently. They needed to understand what she was going to say next.

"If the army comes, we're going to throw ourselves at their feet. Do you understand? We're going to thank them. Every soldier wants to be a hero, and we're going to give them that chance. Do you understand?"

Alarmed, all three nodded.

"Now…your father. He's a member of the Socialist Party. We

don't know how Colonel Gardner feels about that. If we need to, we are going to lie. If we need to, we will no longer be the Esquival family. We will be the Sepulvedas'. If you need to, you're going to tell them that you don't know me. That you don't know your father. Do you understand?"

"Mother?" one of them responded.

"No. No. If you have to, you're going to give me up for your-selves."

"I...I don't want that," Victoria whined. Emelda took selfish comfort in hearing the need in her daughter's voice. She was still a mother. No matter how hard the world was, she was still a mother.

"I know, baby. I know."

She held them. She held all three of them. It was good to feel them.

The radio was quiet. The guns were too.

Finally she let them go and slowly wiped her face.

"About the...ghosts, ghosts is the only word I have. We can't go into the forest, but they can come in. We don't have anything to keep them out. Téa"—she looked at her youngest—"you were very smart and very brave to tell them to go away like that. That's what you all need to do. If you see them, just tell them to go away, okay?"

They nodded.

"Edward...they tried to hurt you. Can you tell me anything else? About the ghosts, the woman in the river?"

"The shadow," Victoria interjected.

Emelda stopped.

"I didn't feel afraid of the children. But the shadow...it was like looking at a moving mountain, something so big and so tall. That feeling of being...amazed, I guess. But it was *alive*. It made me afraid. So afraid that it feels like being scared of anything else is a waste of time."

This was Victoria? This was her little girl? Who wept during thunderstorms and couldn't even talk about the night? "Do you have any idea what it is?"

Victoria thought. "No. But it scares me. It feels...like the devil. Like everything bad in the world looking at you at once."

"It reminded me of Dragón."

Emelda turned abruptly to Edward. "Of Holcomb's *dog*?"

"Yeah...the legends of 'the devil hound'? It felt like that."

"What else? What else can you two tell me about what happened?"

Edward's eyes lit up. "All the tombstones had the same last name. 'Salazar.' Except one. It said...'Holcomb.'"

"'Salazar.'" Emelda's mind went electric.

She walked them quickly up the stairs, past the closed doors and to the bedroom on the third floor. The wardrobe was still pushed aside, letting the dank smell of the secret room pour out. They approached it deliberately, but Edward suddenly stopped.

Emelda looked back to her son.

His eyes were wide, focused on the woman in the paintings.

"That's her," he said. "That's the woman in the river. The one who tried to kill me."

"Eddie..." Her voice was quiet, terrified and confused. "Are you sure?"

"Yes. She had the same blond hair. And...I'll never forget her eyes. How they were so warm and kind even when—"

He gulped. "Even when I couldn't breathe."

Emelda turned to the window, hoping that she could find some indication of what was going on in Rio Rojo. She saw distant smoke, scattered fires, but little else was visible as the day faded to dusk.

Silently, she prayed that William came home soon.

***

Christopher hadn't moved from his bed since he'd come back into Casa Verde.

Just the day before he had felt in control, felt strong and stable even as the world was falling apart. It had been easy to be strong, when it only meant being strong for someone else. But now his hands felt heavy. His *eyes* felt heavy.

He just killed a man. He'd killed a man, and it didn't feel right.

He heard his mother and siblings moving around the house. He didn't care, it didn't matter. Something inside him, some inner light that could keep him going, was gone.

The worst part was, he didn't know if he regretted what had happened.

"Regret" wasn't the right word. A man was dead. But had he deserved to die? Executed, but what right did Christopher have to be executioner?

He wasn't regretful. He was *horrified*. With himself. With what he'd seen and what he'd done. He had told himself he would be ready to kill for self-defense, or for defending someone else. But what had happened in the forest wasn't that at all.

What was it?

His light was going out, and something else was eating him from the newly hollowed space inside. Something dark, cold, and callous. He was realizing how much he hated himself. How long he'd hated himself. He was naïve to think only a few days in Rio Rojo, one stupid adolescent infatuation and a crisis, could change who he was. Inside, he was still the little boy who hated himself. Who was jealous of his little brother, suspicious of his mother.

But that wasn't true either.

He was worse than that.

Because he'd killed a man. After dirt was rubbed in the man's face, he'd killed him.

There was no more wondering about the horrible things people could do each other, as if it were an abstract question. He'd done it.

As the sun set outside his window, he only grew heavier. Would his mother come to look for him, or was she too preoccupied with the younger kids? Would his father come find him, or was he too busy fighting for their lives? Even as bitter, as tired and cold as he was, he knew it was unfair to expect his siblings to think of him. He was selfish. He was awful. And he knew it.

The world could go on, could end without him.

The sky finally went black and he turned over.

The house was quiet. Maybe Mother and everyone else was staying up. Maybe they had rifles in their hands. Maybe they were looking for something. Or maybe they were caught up in themselves, just like he was.

When he fell asleep, he didn't dream. It was only a long moment of darkness and silence. A peaceful wordlessness that was too sweet to last forever.

When he woke up, Alma Sales was with him.

He wasn't sure what sort of comfort came from seeing her. He remembered her hands on his, pressing down so that the gun would fire from his hands. But her skin was smooth, and her short black hair seemed to glitter with soft blue stars in the dark. She still wore her uniform, the thing she had made him kill in. But her smile woke something up in him, some emotion beneath the hate that still stirred inside.

"How'd you get in my room?" he asked, finding he couldn't recognize his own voice.

She kept smiling at him. There was a pity there, an understanding.

The bed balked beneath her as she sat down beside him. She touched his shoulder, but he felt nothing. "María Martin and several others entrusted me with caring for Casa Verde while it was unoccupied. I have a key."

"Oh," he responded.

"Will you come with me?"

"Where?"

"Down to the river."

He looked at her, confused. But she kept smiling.

"I...I know today was difficult. I was raised in this town, raised to expect violence. To commit violence. You were not. I am sorry."

He didn't look at her.

"Will you come with me?"

"I have nowhere else to go, do I?"

She didn't say anything in response.

"I won't be able to leave Rio Rojo, will I?" he asked.

"Do you want to?"

"I'm not sure."

It was true. Even after all of this, he didn't know.

"I need you to be willing to come with me. I won't ever make you do anything you don't want to again."

He stood up, slowly.

She grinned sadly, and took his hand in hers.

***

The ache in William's head was turning hot and searing. The skin around his eyes was burned from salt, and the knot in his stomach had twisted and grown into every part of his body.

He was surprised at how well he adjusted to seeing in the dark, how the whole world now seemed black-and-white under the shining moon. People had conducted their warfare at night for centuries, and it seemed that the bloodshed in Rio Rojo would be no different.

To his horror, William now knew that there was at least one thing Antonio hadn't been lying about.

The Holy Swords in Rio Rojo.

There was no mistaking them. Two men with khaki uniforms, long rifles, and slow, uneasy steps. From the way they moved, William could tell they were scared, young and uncertain. He couldn't see their faces, black silhouettes in the grey light, but he was more than familiar with how the Holy Swords recruited students from college campuses. If these two were over twenty, they would be promoted up the ranks swiftly.

They were idealistic, foolish. Zealous. Molded into killers by Pasqual and his promises of paradise on earth born of wading through blood. It would be much simpler, William knew, to move in the woods if they would just remove their armbands, scarlet red things with brilliant white crosses.

It was no way to hide within a population. No way to be a fish in water.

They moved in the direction of Casa Verde, and William followed slowly behind them. The glowing children, the ghosts, had left him long ago.

Now he was alone, and in the quiet he could hear that the guerillas had water canteens at their sides. The sloshing became hypnotic, soothing.

He needed to figure out how to kill these boys for their water. And how to do it quietly, without firing a shot that would alert anyone else to his position.

"Do you think the rest of them are dead?" he heard one ask the other.

"I...probably."

Their voices were soft, deceptively so. But William knew killers with softer, kinder voices.

"They didn't tell us that the population would be ready."

"I don't think they knew."

"No…but who do you think killed that old woman?"

William kept quiet, kept moving slowly. But now he was listening intently, paying more mind to their words than to the carefulness of his steps. His foot fell on a tangle of branches.

The boys stopped. William kept still.

He was far enough away, in thick enough vines, that they wouldn't be able to see the dark outline of a man. But he stopped breathing, afraid that even the smallest noise would result in these children, these unrefined murderers, firing their guns into the woods.

"I think someone in the town knew we were here. I think they killed her to get them going. To scare them into a frenzy."

"Well, it fucking *worked*," the other said. "Did you see those kids? Riding horses?"

"If we make it out alive, I'm going to have nightmares for the rest of my life. I didn't think people actually *smiled* when they killed each other. I never enjoyed it, anyway."

There was nothing like the enormity of death that made every idea, every conviction and every sacred thought seem small. Whatever massacre these boys had escaped, William imagined that they were revolutionaries no longer.

A bullet shot out from the woods.

One of the boys dropped to his knees and collapsed. The other screamed, but only for a moment.

William crouched low to the ground, hoping that the gunshots and whatever came after would deafen any noise he could make.

Two more forms emerged from the woods: one tall, and the other much shorter.

A match lit up, and William could see their faces. Two young boys, possibly only a little older than Christopher.

The shorter one brought his match to a kerosene lamp, and in the light the two surveyed the corpses carefully. They removed the rifles, the pistols and knives. They patted down every pocket, every part of the men.

The taller one removed what looked like a book, a small thing that he held between his thumb and index finger.

He looked it over, flipping through the pages before he laughed and tossed it aside. "Communist trash."

"Come on, there may be more of them," the shorter answered.

"Do you really think so? After how much we've done today?"

"Who knows?" the shorter answered with little emotion in his voice. "But they told us the more we kill, the more favors we get."

"Right."

The kerosene lamp went out, and for long seconds William was blind again. When his sight came back, he still waited, careful to make sure that he heard no footsteps or breathing.

He approached the corpses, desperate and tired. Bloody water canteens were still at their sides.

William took one and opened it quickly. The water hit his empty, swirling stomach in painful waves.

***

Under the moon, Christopher could see Alma clearly.

Each step he took with her only made him more tired. The pressure behind his eyes was unbearable. Where he had once been empty, he was now full of emotions. He was afraid. He was sad.

As they walked through the forest, the children of the woods peered out at them. In the calm, they seemed like earthbound stars, brilliant faces that brought some small comfort in their smiles.

He stumbled over a rock or root, and Alma offered him her hand. He took it gingerly, and felt a relief that he could lean on someone.

For a long while, the earth was kind and quiet. The bugs, the birds and bullets stopped. There was only the cool, humid night slicking his skin. Only wet leaves brushing against his side as they walked.

Alma said nothing, and he offered nothing in return.

Steadily, the gurgling sounds of the running river rose up to meet them.

In the moonlight, the river didn't seem red or bloody. It was any other dark, cool water, spilt with stars and the blue-white moon. Alma led him down to the shore, and sat down on the wet sand. He sat with her, and looked to the water.

"No one is born to do what we did today. You know that, right?" Alma spoke tenderly.

Christopher didn't say anything, because he wasn't sure what to say at all.

Alma took a handful of wet dirt in her hands and began molding it into a perfect sphere.

"Maybe killing is inevitable. But it's not natural. You have to be educated, groomed for it. In the army's elite forces, you have to care for a puppy for four months. You sleep with it, eat with it. And then, they make you kill it."

"That's horrible," Christopher said. But there was no outrage in his voice, no disgust. It was simply a statement of fact.

"It is," Alma said. "I've always found it awful, anyway. Personally, I think it's easier to kill a man than a dog. Dogs only know love. Kindness. Their existence is an easier, painless one."

"Men can love too," Christopher said in response.

Alma chuckled. "Yes, I suppose they can."

The river continued running.

Alma threw her perfect ball of wet dirt into the water, making it land with a squelch that sent up droplets like dirty pearls against the sky.

"You know how you feel is natural, right?" she asked meekly.

She sounded like anyone else, any other concerned friend, Christopher thought. Not like a killer, the leader of a death squad. She was being tender, patient, but she was responsible for how he felt. She'd held his hand and guided him through the execution. But where was his anger? His sense of betrayal?

"I don't know how I feel," he responded.

"Do you want to *try* telling me, at least?"

He looked at the river, at the dark and distant trees across the streaming starlight.

"I feel small," he said.

"What do you mean?"

"I…I feel like I'm not any different from the man I—"

"We," she corrected.

"*We* killed. I feel empty. Useless."

"Useless?" she asked.

"Useless," he said back. "The world is only getting worse, and I can't do anything. I hate myself. I hate myself so much."

"Why?" she asked.

"Because I'm still angry. I'm still bitter and still scared."

"Who are you angry with?"

"Me!" But the moment the word came out of his mouth, so did the tears. The levee in his heart broke, and with it all the feelings he thought were gone welled up. He tried to pull his face into his knees, but Alma guided him to her shoulder. He couldn't resist, couldn't fight her. He just wept as she ran her fingers along his back.

"You're mad at yourself for feeling bad about killing a man?"

"Yes," he offered back between sputtering breaths.

"Is that all, though?"

"N-no. I'm angry with myself because I can't change things. I'm so small. I'm so *fucking* small."

He tried to keep his weeping quiet. There were no more gunshots in the air, but there could still be insurgents in the woods.

"Who do you want to be strong for, Christopher?" Alma asked him.

He wept so much, he couldn't breathe.

"Who do you want to change for?"

"Everyone!" he yelled back. "My parents, my brother and sisters. You."

Alma laughed with a bit of relief. "Yes, me. But what about you? Do you want to be stronger for yourself?"

"Wuh-what?"

"Do you want to be strong for yourself? Happy for yourself?"

"I—"

"You need to be *certain*, Christopher. You *must* be certain. Strong people must be strong not just for other people. It's easy to be relied on. To be needed. It's an entirely different thing to be strong alone."

"Why do I need to be strong alone? I don't want to be alone!"

She brought her hand to his cheek. It was so warm, so soft.

He looked in her eyes. To her lips.

"You aren't."

She kissed him lightly.

And she kissed him again.

She guided his hand to the back of her neck.

He could smell her now. Earthy, flowery.

"You aren't alone, Christopher, you are here. You are with me." Her hands were at his chest. "You're here with me."

Everything seemed brighter, clearer. He could see her now, better than he ever had before. The world was lighter without his clothes, and now the starlight of the river glittered against her.

She took his hand to the water.

They waded in, the cool dark running up to their waists.

She smiled at him. "Do you want to be stronger for yourself, Christopher?"

"I—"

But looking at her, he couldn't help but feel stronger. He would make himself into whatever he needed for her.

He walked to her and cupped her face in his hands.

She leaned into him. Their warmth came together.

His body was burning, every nerve twitching and electric.

His mind spun. Kept spinning.

Alma and the river were everything. Running against him, cold and heat at once sliding across every part of his being.

There was a moment where it all stopped. An isolated second where everything stood still.

And after, Alma smiled.

The river resumed its running.

The birds went back to singing.

Christopher wanted to laugh and cry at once.

But the river ran faster. Something swept his legs. Something pulled him deep. And Alma rose above him, a smile like no other on her face. He screamed, but the water filled his mouth. And beneath the current, hands caressed him while the dark water took him whole.

***

Emelda held the rifle Christopher left behind in her hands.

She hated herself for not realizing that he was gone earlier. She could have sworn she saw him come in when she went up the stairs with the older children, that he had gone off for much-needed rest. But when she went into his room, he was gone.

She ran throughout the house, calling his name. Edward and Victoria went looking for him too, shouting with cupped hands around their mouths.

By the time the sun went down, their throats were haggard and worn.

Edward had his father's pistol, though the holster looked awkward and heavy at his side.

Emelda took them to the kitchen. The carving knives were in a block, and she removed three of them.

"Careful," she told Edward and Victoria. "Don't cut yourselves. And Téa—"

Téa looked up, confused and scared, lips just moments away from trembling.

"Don't touch these unless you have to. And if you have to… you do what you need to and *run*. Okay?"

"Mommy." Téa was so close to crying again. "Where's Christopher?"

"I don't know, honey."

"He said he was gonna be strong for us, but he isn't here!"

"I know. I know he's not here. Daddy's not here either. But you are. You're my whole world right now. And that means I have to worry about *you*, okay?"

Téa sniffled and threw herself towards her mother's legs.

"Christopher has a girlfriend, I think. He probably went to check on her."

"He has a *girlfriend*?" Edward asked.

"From what I can tell." Emelda smiled as she stroked Téa's hair. "Her name is 'Alma Sales,' pretty girl too."

Edward smiled.

Emelda prayed that was the case, that Christopher had been persuaded by some stupid boy's notion of heroism to ride off searching for Alma Sales. Her impression of the girl was that she could more than take care of herself, but boys always believed they needed to sacrifice themselves for perfectly capable women. If her son was a stupid man, she could correct him. She could smack him across his forehead, yell at him for being reckless, foolish and sweet. She could throw herself at him, and howl into his shoulders as she wept in relief.

If he was a stupid man, he could be corrected. But there would be no changing a dead man.

She prayed, fiercely, for the return of her oldest child.

Please, let him have found William out there in the jungle. Please, let them both come through the door at any minute.

But the minutes became long hours. The children needed to eat. *She* needed to eat.

Emelda scavenged for bread and cheese. She cut them up for her children and made them sit at the little table in the servants' quarters. She ate slowly, not tasting the food but eating because her stomach was in a desperate, miserable pain.

She hadn't heard gunshots for some time. She hoped this meant the town was still now, that whatever gruesome labor that had needed doing was done. The radio, too, had been silent for hours. No word from Gardner, no pronouncements of the dead or the guilty.

But the silence was pregnant with dread, and Emelda couldn't stop expecting that something awful was coming next. She hadn't forgotten that ghosts were real now. There was no telling what else was out there, waiting for her to drop her guard.

"I wonder," Edward started. "Do you think we could move somewhere colder? I've always wondered what snow felt like."

Emelda considered it. "Is that what you would want?"

"I don't know," Edward said.

"I'd like to move closer to a coast," Victoria said.

Emelda laughed. "And what about you, Téa? If you could live anywhere in the world, where it would be?"

"Our old apartment back in Margería," Téa said sadly.

Her daughter may as well have punched her in the stomach.

"Things were easier there. I was *happier* there."

"I...me too, baby. I was happier too."

Gardner's voice interrupted them over the radio. "Countrymen and patriots."

The colonel's voice still sent shivers down Emelda's spine. There was a kindness in it, but only a surface-level kindness. Even without a television screen, she could visualize his smile, a disinterested doctor delivering a fatal diagnosis with tenderness to avoid any outburst of emotion from their patient. Just beneath the kindness was something darker: the low, bemused growling of a tiger content that it was near everything it could ever want.

"Our forces have retaken Margería. The capital is under control and the communists are on the run. However, we are aware of new regional concentrations of forces in the following areas: Bosque Bautismal, Indirrí, and Rio Rojo.

"To the residents of Bosque Bautismal, Indirrí, and Rio Rojo: we urge you to stay inside your homes in the coming hours. As interim commander of the armed forces, I am announcing the full deployment of our nation's glorious army, navy and air force against this internal threat. I authorize the citizens of the affected areas to form self-defense squads, who may cooperate under the full command of the armed forces. In this moment, Antioch calls upon us all to be heroes. I know you are hurting, and I know you are scared. But I affirm now, as I will always affirm to you, that I hurt alongside you, brothers and sisters.

"Hold fast, and stay strong. Long live our Republic."

And the radio went quiet once more.

Their best hope was on its way, but she felt no more hopeful now than before.

Emelda looked out into the night, knowing that monsters were walking between the trees.

***

William hadn't meant to fall asleep. He hadn't even meant to close his eyes. His stomach hurt from the water. His body was cool, but his stomach hurt.

He rushed up and quietly relieved himself.

The corpses of the two communists were still nearby. Seeing them clearly, how young they were, his heart sank a little more. Both had beard-stubble shadows, both had wide eyes that still looked out into the forest. Gingerly as he could, William reached down to close them.

When he looked back up, a glowing face stared out from the forest. He lingered on it a little longer, finding it wouldn't turn away from him. When he walked forward, it didn't step back.

The boy looked no older than six, with dark hair covered in leaves and eyes darker than the world around him. Cradled in his arms were fruits, berries, and yucca.

William looked at the boy skeptically.

"Please," the ghost said.

William reached out and took the food in his hands.

"You're a father," the boy said.

William balked.

"You're a father...and you want your family. But we're all family here."

"What do you mean?"

The boy smiled. "We're all from the same dirt, aren't we?"

Before he could answer, William heard the thunderous clapping of horse hooves.

The boy receded into the dark, and William was alone again.

***

Statement from the Armed Forces of Antioch to the Leadership of the Interim Military Junta:

The Armed Forces wishes to assure the people of Antioch that the restoration of internal order and peace is the foremost mission of our ranks. To achieve these goals, the police of Margería have been disbanded and replaced with the military police. New recruits from the police academies will fall under the command of MP, who will train them in combat as well as police work. These units will first be deployed to Bosque Bautismal, where reliable intelligence suggests the author Umberto Santrich has organized an insurgency.

The threat environment of Rio Rojo is more complex, and will require a multifaceted response. The population of Rio Rojo is well-armed, and traditionally hostile to interference from the central government. Latest evidence suggests that Senator William Esquival, the last recognized descendent of Thomas Holcomb other than his four children, has retreated there and is residing in the Holcomb family house. We cannot discount theories that Senator Esquival's presence, or perhaps even leadership, will embolden communist insurgents. And Senator María Martin likewise is in the region.

What follows is the proposal for a rapid invasion of Rio Rojo. "Operación Dragón."

RECLÁIMING

The blackberries were ripe, sweet and bitter. The juice streamed out of the corners of William's mouth, making his dark stubble sticky. It was only after the first berry that he realized how hungry he was. He was far older now than he had been in the army, and had noticed even standing for long hours was painful. Whatever endurance he had left was only motivated by a fierce, unrelenting desire to ensure that his children would live longer than he would.

There would be no forgiving himself, no redeeming himself, if he arrived to a bloodied and ruined Casa Verde. After seeing the slaughter in Rio Rojo, he could not discount the brutality of these people.

But still, some demonic doubts whispered and lingered: "If there is truly a conspiracy against your family, the conspirators have horses. They will have noticed Antonio has vanished. They may be younger, more able-bodied, and heavily armed. The plot is already in motion, and you're pushing yourself towards dying more miserably. It would be easier to lie down. To rest. There will be plenty of time for someone else's sons to bury you."

A mix of fear and adrenaline kept him moving even as the horse patrols grew more regular. The executioners were growing bolder, carrying lanterns at their sides as they patrolled the mountain paths. When they called out to each other, William only heard some voices which had finished puberty. The rest were high-pitched or cracking, laughing and singing as they rode across the mountains for stragglers and survivors.

When he could see them, illuminated by the faint yellow light of their lanterns, he could see acne, smiles, and feral eyes. They were boys and girls both, challenging each other to kill more. Never before had he seen child soldiers, and now he found them far more terrifying than any army.

They were anarchic, dragging bodies behind them, painting their faces with blood. If these children caught him, they would kill him.

He moved even slower now, even more painfully.

William knew that in all likelihood, they had already reached Casa Verde. But he couldn't accept this, the reality that every step forward was useless. That he would die somewhere without his wife.

That was it. That was his motivation. If he was going to die, it would be with his wife. He would get back to her. He would get back to all of them.

The children on horseback continued to patrol, and when they came close he would fall to the ground. Sometimes they would say important things. As wild as they seemed, they spoke of "orders" and "plans." The name "Alma" came up often. William thought back to when they'd first arrived in Rio Rojo, and the young woman with the long rifle on her back. He understood now that she was the leader of this band of murderers.

A sixteen-year-old girl.

A boy on horseback came close, and William crouched again.

The boy stopped. He had a wispy mustache and deep lines on his forehead. William studied him in full detail, hoping he would move on.

But the boy's dark eyes met William's.

Quickly, mechanically, William shot up and fired a single shot towards the boy's chest. The bullet sent the boy flying off his horse, which whinnied ahead in wild fright.

William ran forward, gun trained on the motionless body. The boy was still breathing, though blood was dribbling out of the corners of his mouth.

There was a knife at his side. William took the boy's knife.

Fear. Hate. Every bitter animal emotion in his eyes.

"I'm sorry."

There was a long, neat cut across the throat.

William took the boy's knife and his water, and looked up the path.

The horse was still there. Startled, stamping its feet, but still there.

William approached it slowly, humming low to calm it. It breathed quickly, a sound like a scream escaping its mouth. He held up his arms and waited. The creature, accustomed to people, incomplete without a rider, calmed down. He ran his hand through its mane and smiled.

Then, mounting the horse despite every pain in his body, he pulled its reins and squeezed its sides.

***

Edward listened carefully when his mother described what the army's arrival in Rio Rojo might look like.

If they were lucky, she explained, the army would be received with no resistance from people in the town. In this case, they would cooperate with the army and simply wait. If the situation across the country stabilized, then maybe there would be a chance that they could leave Rio Rojo and Antioch peacefully.

However, if people in the town tried to shoot the army, tried to fight them, they were going to wait for the fighting to be over. No matter how good the militiamen in Rio Rojo thought they were with guns, they would be overwhelmed by a force that could fire cannons from the river or fire mortars into the mountains.

Mother told them they would surrender themselves. They would introduce themselves as "the family of a retired officer." If William was with them, they would follow their father's lead.

"Your father is the most emotionally intelligent man I've ever met," she explained, "If anyone can appeal to a man's soul, it's William Esquival."

Edward knew his father was good with people. He had all sorts of friends, and all sorts of people who paid them visits. His father knew the names of the baker in their neighborhood, the man who shined shoes, and the owners of several nearby cafés. Father sometimes introduced people as "my good friend and political foe" and would have them over to dinner. He did this because he believed "knowing a man helps him know you."

But would he be able to save them from this?

Now they sat close to the radio. Edward crossed his legs, keenly aware of the knife on the table behind him. It was strange, but he was relaxed now. It was as if knowing the terror, fully sharing and shaping it with words, limited it, gave it confines and contours that it could not cross. The woman in the river was only a ghost. The communists, the army, were only people with guns.

"Are you okay?"

He looked over to Torie. "Yeah," he said.

"Do you think Father will make it back? Or Christopher?"

He turned around to his mother. Emelda looked at him too, as unable to provide an answer as anyone else.

"I do," he said after thinking.

"I do too," Torie said.

Edward sighed. His mother smiled.

There was a knock at the door.

It echoed loudly, filling the air just as much as any explosion. Edward waited, hoping with all his heart that it was only his imagination, that there were no more ghosts outside.

But the knocking came again.

"Edward," Emelda growled. "Take your sisters and hide."

"Mom, let me go with you," he offered.

"No. Not today. If anything happens, you take care of them, do you hear me?"

She turned to him with softest, most tender smile she had ever given him. She leaned down and placed a hand on his cheek.

"You know, I've been harder on you than I mean to be. And it's only now that I realize why...I see the good in your father in you. That kind, tireless goodness. Always running to help other people so much that he doesn't stop to help himself. But son, there's no more worrying about me. Or your dad. Or Christopher. From now, until we are safe, the only people you care about, the only people in your whole world, are the people whose hands you can hold. Do you understand?"

So many indistinct images welled in his mind. Mother, dragged from the house screaming. Father, dead in the woods somewhere. Christopher with a bleeding wound in his head. He thought about shadows, about the woman from the river dragging him down into the water. As much as he believed he was done being afraid, the thought of losing his mother brought his fears back. Losing her had never been a possibility, never even been a thought.

"Son?"

"Okay, Mother. Okay."

He couldn't look at her as he turned to his sisters.

They grabbed the knives, the pistol. They needed to hide somewhere on the first floor, where they could run out of the house if they needed. He found a servants' bedroom, a room with a window that they would break if they needed to. The room was plain, unpainted wood that still smelled sweet after all the time it had been left to stand in the swamp's humidity.

Téa sat on the bed and sighed, but shot up and pointed out the window. "They're outside."

Edward followed his sister's finger.

"Is it the kids from the forest?" Torie asked, straining her eyes.

Nothing out in the night was glowing. No pale faces looked back.

But Edward caught the glint of the moon off a metal rifle. The shadow of a man with a gun.

***

Emelda tensed herself and raised the rifle.

She stepped back from the door after turning the knob, throwing it back so she could fire if the person on the other side had a weapon.

But the figure on the door was an old woman, with gun-metal grey hair and a wry, lupine smile.

"...María?" Emelda almost gasped between syllables.

"Emelda," María Martin responded sweetly.

María wore a black dress, the very same she'd worn when she'd buried her sons and husband.

"Antonio said they killed you!" Emelda shrieked.

"Oh, dearest." María stepped forward, into the house and towards Emelda. "Please." She motioned to the rifle. "Please put that down. You'll hurt me with that thing if you're not careful."

Emelda lowered the rifle. "You're not dead?"

María laughed, "It would be quite a thing to be here if I was, but then I wouldn't be the first dead woman to terrify your family, would I?"

Then she sighed, a sad look entering her eyes. "We're both mothers, Emelda. And I've come here to tell you some things you need to know. Things I think you would only understand coming from another mother. Can we sit? Do you have any tea?"

"Tea?"

"Right. Right." María waved her hand, as if acknowledging that the request was difficult, if not absurd. "I forget that that these aren't normal times anymore. Which is a pity."

"How are you not dead? Antonio said they found your corpse."

María sneered. "Please, Emelda. I may not be dead, but I *am* old. My joints hurt from coming up this hill and I've come such a long way to see you. Please, let us sit while we talk."

María walked as if she knew her way around the house, leaving Emelda behind in the dark entry room. Emelda followed eventually, slowly, mystified. Seeing María alive took the world from beneath her feet. She had been so certain that the old woman was dead. Antonio had cried *real* tears. And the description of María's mutilated, hanging corpse had made her nauseous. She'd regretted her harsh parting words with the old woman in that moment, imaging how scared she must have been in her dying moments.

But here María was, sitting on her couch. Smiling.

"You ask how I am not dead? I believe someone has played a foul trick on the people of this town. The awful truth is that if you take an old woman, beat and bloody her so much that her face is unrecognizable, she'll look like any other old woman's corpse."

"Why would you not just tell them, then? That you're alive. Do you know how many people they're killing out there?"

"I am afraid, honestly."

"Afraid of them?"

"No, Emelda. I'm afraid they would stop."

"I—"

"You know, I do love you. And I do love your husband. I'd like this world to be a place for people like you, but it's not. It's a place for people like me."

María leaned back into the couch and breathed deeply through her nose. Then, as if well rested, she came back up and leaned forward. "The truth is that a cancer has existed in this country for a very long time. And it is a deadly, awful cancer that has spread throughout this nation's body. The cancer may have many names. 'Liberal democracy,' 'enlightenment,' 'socialism' or... 'communism.' But it is all the same cancer. The cancer of weakness. And now, now the cancer is being treated."

"Innocent people could be getting caught up in this!"

"Innocent people get caught up in any great moment, dear. Why would they fare any better in this one?"

"So you're not dead, but you faked your death. All to whip people up into a killing frenzy?" Emelda asked.

"No, no, not for that."

María put her hands together like a temple. There was a sense of gravity in her eyes, as if she were about impart some sacred, coveted secret.

"It is time you and I have an earnest talk, Emelda. About Elizabeth *Holcomb* and her child with Thomas. About myself, and about Colonel Gardner."

***

William kept the horse moving steadily towards Casa Verde. Moving faster somehow felt unbearably slow, the knowledge that he could get back to his family faster both frustrating and tantalizing. But he knew that if he came across another rider, he would have no choice other than to fight. He had seen these children kill, and having already killed two people in one day, he wanted to hold his children with as little blood on his hands as possible.

If they saw him, they would shoot. It would be more noise and greater attention to himself. He had come too far to be executed.

The ghostly faces of the forest children peered out from the darkness only occasionally now. Their faces were sullen and mournful, stripped of the smiles and curiosity that they had held before. They sat in the branches, hung tight to tree trunks, and poked out from bushes.

The woods were full of dead children, William mused, and they would be filled with so many more. Antonio called them "covenants," but William had spent little time wondering about their nature. Christopher had called them "ghosts," but he had just ignored his son. The world seemed too complicated for ghosts, but here they were.

He and Emelda had bonded over suffering and hardship. They had never spoken about it, but it was true. Emelda's experiences with death and the dying had come long after his; when he became a public defender he had been removed from the battlefield for over five years. But when Emelda became a doctor, for the first time she saw a man bleed out. They'd never said out loud that they shared this, the intimate knowledge that came with witnessing the enormity of death.

But they responded to death and crises the same way. They distanced themselves and created plans on how to respond. In crises, William reverted back to planning his solutions step-by-step, connecting the pieces in one singular, attainable chain. It made him an effective legislator, a "problem-solver" who could form a coalition of willing parties.

As absurd as it was, the ghosts could wait.

William could finally see lights from Casa Verde's windows. The house stood out starkly in the dark, with its medieval towers and wide porches. The windows filled with dim yellow, the color of a sleepy, exhausted light.

His heart fluttered at the thought of Emelda sleeping, cradling her children around her. He would jump from his horse and run to the house, leave the animal to find its own way. He would burst through the door and slam it behind him. He would find Emelda and shake her awake. He would hold her tight, and he would never let go.

Excitedly, he leapt down from his horse and ran.

All the pain melted away, replaced by wonderful, rapturous euphoria. All that mattered to him in the whole world was in that house. The five most important people in existence. The ghosts didn't matter. The guns didn't matter. What mattered were those small hands he could take in his own. What mattered was staying awake so his children could sleep. What mattered were Sunday breakfasts, cleaning scraped knees, and long nights explaining what it meant to grow up. What mattered was watching his children become men and women of their own, watching and helping them as they fell in and out of love until they found the sort of love he shared with Emelda.

What mattered was Emelda. Not the ache in his knees or the blood in his throat.

Emelda.

He ran and the world faded away. Only the house existed now. Only the house mattered now. Not the woods around the grounds, or the armed men and women who stalked those grounds.

The bullet entered his shoulder.

William collapsed, knocked down by the force. It burned from the inside as bubble after bubble of dark blood welled up from his own open body. He screamed and thrashed on the ground, but still crawled forward. He could see the double doors, the gardens. It was cruel how close he was! This was unfair, evil.

Two hands grabbed the back of his shirt and hoisted him up.

Two hands pulled him away, the lights inside the house growing dimmer and smaller.

"No!" he cried out. He fought back, coming to his knees and leaping forward.

Rifle butts rammed into his chest, knocking the wind and spit out of him as his ribs cracked beneath them.

"Please." William wept desperately now. "Please just let me be with my family."

There were so many little details that came to him then. When Christopher first came home, he had been so small. Just a little red-pink thing. William remembered calling his first son a "gumball," and how Emelda had playfully frowned. He remembered Christopher, proud of his grades, eager to show off. How proud *he* had been, to have made such a happy son.

Edward, so impossibly smart and so brilliantly handsome. His son would just read, unprompted, for hours. Sometimes William would sneak into his room as he slept, and take the books from his bed and move them so he didn't roll over them.

William was afraid of Torie growing up, of learning that there were worse things in the world than the dark. But he also remembered the way she was kind, the way she was sensitive, and recognized that within that sensitivity there was a will to fight for what was right.

Téa…he hardly knew his youngest daughter. He knew she laughed at dogs, that she loved them and wanted a puppy of their own. He'd wanted to get her one, before the world fell away.

"Please just let me!" he called out again.

Let him go. Let him buy his family a puppy. Let them have Christmas in some distant country, somewhere with snow and lights. Emelda would make them coffee in the morning as they waited for Téa to wake up. She would squeal and scream at the puppy in her mother's hands. And then, as the younger children fawned over the puppy, William would pull his eldest aside. He would give him a simple gift, but one he hoped would mean a lot. His uncle's police badge, the only thing William still had from his older brother.

He would tell his son, "Part of being a good man is being

happy with the sacrifices you make for others." It was the defining lesson William had learned from his older brother, the first man to sacrifice so much for him.

"Please," William whimpered now.

But now Casa Verde itself denied him. Its long porches, high walls, its ivy-covered towers, looked down on him as if in disgust. Unknown hands tied his wrists behind a tree. Another pressed into his shoulder to stop the bleeding.

"Senator Esquival."

William turned to the speaker. A pretty young woman, with short black hair and a soft smile. She wore a khaki uniform, with a long bloody knife at her side and a rifle slung across her back.

"Alma," he said.

She nodded. "Yes, Senator."

"Alma...I need to get to my family. They're in danger. Someone's going to hurt them."

He would appeal to her. She liked Christopher, so she couldn't be a bad person. Just a misguided child, indoctrinated by violence.

"Yes," Alma said kindly, as if soothing a patient through bad news, "but only *once*. Only once, and they'll never hurt again."

"What?"

She knelt down to him. She found a piece of cloth and dampened it with water. She cleaned his face, and suddenly William felt cool and new.

"You've hurt much longer than you ever needed to, Senator. For this, I am truly sorry."

"Alma—"

But the young woman backed away, receding behind him and away from his line of sight. Now it was just him and the house. The distant, uncaring house.

Then, coming from the side of the house, he saw a man with

a gun. As the man approached, he seemed to grow impossibly larger. William could make out narrow shoulders and long hair. But there was something behind him, a towering, indistinct thing that curled like a mass of black flames.

Something in that twisting shape held his attention, mesmerized him.

When the man came close enough, William gasped.

His brown hair was curled. His eyes were brilliant green. There was no mistaking Thomas Holcomb, the face that had looked down on them from countless portraits inside Casa Verde.

And there was something else too.

The shape of the nose, the contours of his chin. Something familiar beneath the likeness to Holcomb.

The man raised his rifle.

"Christopher?"

***

Emelda heard two gunshots.

At the first, María merely smiled. At the second, which passed a few minutes later, she nodded.

"What's going on outside?" Emelda asked coldly.

"You could say that I have something of a praetorian guard. I brought them with me to protect us while we talk."

"What did you come here to talk about?"

María laughed. "Emelda, we are two grown women, alone in a massive house as the world falls apart on a dark night. I propose we talk about what people *always* talk about in our situation."

A cruel, wry gleam entered her eyes. "I propose we talk about *ghost stories.*"

"The children in the woods—"

"Yes, them, but so much more…this won't do, Emelda. I know

this house like the back of my hand, I'm going to make us tea."

Emelda was shaking. Fear, rage, indignation. "I don't have time for your bullshit, María, this is my home and—"

At this, María laughed. A roaring, deep, cruel sound.

"You stupid little girl. If anything should be abundantly clear by now, it should be that this is *not* your home. And it never was."

Shock. Shock as if María had smacked her across the face. Worse, because it implied that she had no ownership of the space where her children slept, the space where she could protect them the most.

But María left her, standing there as she walked to the kitchen and began making tea.

"If you come wait with me," María called out, "I can start answering your questions. There are some things you need to know, but I'd like to know what you know first."

Emelda walked into the kitchen, but not of her own free will. She was dejected, realizing she simply had no other choice. María had every advantage, every power over her. She was at the mercy of this woman. She had been ever since William had accepted María's invitation.

"Ask away, Emelda." María didn't even look at her as she boiled water on the stove.

"You mentioned Colonel Gardner. What do you know about him?"

"Heh. Still stuck in the present, are you?" María put a trembling finger to her chin, as if in deep thought. "I can tell you that I've met the colonel on several occasions. I found him to be a promising soldier, maybe even a threat. But I will say that I am impressed by his recent actions. What I wouldn't give to call him my son, Emelda."

"So…are you working with him?"

"Oh no. No, no. The colonel and I want the same thing. This country."

"You want to control Antioch?"

"Please," María spat. The water steamed, and María made her tea. One cup for her, another for Emelda. With trembling hand, she extended one cup to Emelda. Her smile was still sweet and sly.

With no agency of her own, Emelda took her cup.

"Emelda, I've been leading this nation by the nose my entire political career. They may call me a 'relic,' 'the obelisk,' a 'dinosaur.' But there's a reason I outlasted everyone else. 'Controlling' a nation is infinitely more work than 'leading' it. Than 'guiding' or 'molding' it. I suspect Colonel Gardner is in the very first moments of learning this lesson, and I aim to use it for his undoing."

"What's this have to do with my family?"

"Aha. *There's* the mother in you. I'm afraid you won't like my answer. But please, walk with me."

María led her out of the kitchen, through the halls where Thomas Holcomb looked down on them as he always had.

"Thomas Holcomb united a country that was never meant to be united. A lord among warlords. Before him there were small wars, fiefdoms, barons, chiefs and colonizers. Little men bleeding against one another. Holcomb made this country a nation, and he didn't do it alone.

"Miranda Holcomb was his wife. Sure. She gave him children, he gave her this house. By all accounts, a good woman. A good patriot." She turned back to Emelda then, with a sad little look in her eyes. "To be honest, I always felt bad for the poor woman. Mothers, wives. We're always the ones who suffer most for love of country. It asks us to give ourselves, and then our children."

"You can't have my children, María."

María didn't answer. Her silence filled Emelda with dread.

"Miranda Holcomb was his wife, but she wasn't his world. His love. The horrible truth is that there was only one person who Thomas Holcomb loved with his whole being."

"Elizabeth," Emelda guessed.

María nodded.

They walked to the third floor, down the long quiet hallways and into the secret room. The moonlight came through the window in clean blue rays. Elizabeth seemed impossibly sad and pretty, a young girl in love with the man at her side and the child in her arms.

"You know what happened to her, María. You know that she's buried with her whole family in the woods."

"Yes. I do know that."

"The truth is, for all we give for our nation, our Founder gave more."

Nausea welled up in Emelda. "You mean—"

"To create a nation, to give it life and bind it together, it needs to be truly *given life*. The only thing that gives a country meaning is the willingness of people to kill and die beside each other. Oh sure," María laughed, "the songs and the flags are pretty and pleasing. But while culture and arts change, the meaning of a gun and a bullet are constant. More important, though, is the act of feeding a nation itself.

"Colonel Gardner once told me Thomas Holcomb united the country by making covenant with the devil. He was mistaken, but close. It wasn't with the devil, but with *Antioch itself*. And ever since that first secret covenant, the people of Rio Rojo have been careful to maintain our nation. To keep it fed.

"Emelda, you criticized me for sending my children to die. You couldn't possibly know how cruel your words were, how even now they conjure up a rage I've never felt before. How *dare* you speak to me that way?

"You don't know what Miranda felt, what Elizabeth felt. You sure as *hell* don't know what I feel! But you will. And after that, you're going to die just like your husband did.

"Killed by the man who used to be your son."

***

Edward and Torie watched people with guns multiply across the yard of Casa Verde. Slim shadows with long arms, pouring from the woods towards the front of the house. In that direction they heard two gunshots and the ragged, indistinct screaming of a man. After the second shot, the screams stopped.

The pistol was heavy in Edward's hands. There would only be so much he could do with a pistol. There were too many of them now, each of them far better trained and armed than a teenage boy who'd only shot his first targets the day before.

"We need to make a plan," Edward whispered to his sister.

"Yes," Torie whispered back.

Torie pressed Téa against her. Looking at them now, Edward found his sisters impossibly small.

"Senator Martin is in the house with Mom. But there's a reason she hasn't come to get us," Edward began.

"Mother doesn't trust her."

"Right. Then we don't either."

"They're going to the front of the house. That means if we need to, we're going to run out the back. Into the woods."

"What?" A little bit of shock and anger entered Torie's voice. "Eddie, the woman...Elizabeth. She wants *you*. The kids didn't drag me in, but they pulled *you*. I don't want to go anywhere where you're closer to her."

Edward thought of the world going dark. Of suffocating in

blindness. Of being impossibly cold as an iron hand gripped his throat.

"I don't want to, either. But I would rather—" He gulped. "If I have to die, I want you two to live. I want Mom to live. So if they come for me, Torie, I need you to take Téa and run."

He extended the pistol towards her. Torie looked at it, and then up to her brother's face.

"You're a better shot than I am, Torie. And I want you to know…how proud I am of you. How brave I think you are. I need you to know that I love you, okay?"

Edward could see Torie's eyes glisten as she took the pistol. "Edward, I'm so tired of crying. Please don't."

Téa turned towards her big sister with the instinct only very small children have, throwing her arms up around her neck and holding her tight.

"It's gonna be okay," Téa assured them. "It's gonna be okay because we're *all* brave, okay?"

Edward overcame his shock and surprise. "You're right, Téa. I'm sorry if I scared you."

He came to his sisters and held them tight.

In the front of the house, the door started to break.

Edward leapt up. "We need to go now."

"But—" Téa started.

"No," he replied coldly. "If whoever out there was here to help, they wouldn't break down the door. We need to go now."

He grabbed Torie's hand and held his pistol in the other. "Téa, I need you to hold Torie's hand. No matter what happens, you don't let go. Okay?"

"Okay." Her voice was so soft and quiet.

Edward opened the door slowly and peered out. He could hear them at the front of the house, stomping loudly, knocking over furniture and kicking down doors. He caught the sight of one of them, a young woman with short black hair and cold blue eyes.

"Move!" he hissed at his sisters.

He ran. Nothing else existed other than his sisters' hands and the door in the back of the house. Furiously, he ran. And when he came to the door, he threw it open, paying no more mind to noise.

The grass was wet and cold with dark evening dew. The sky was tranquil and bright with the moon.

His mind roared at him. *Don't turn back, don't turn back.*

But Téa stopped. Her scream shook the world.

Edward turned back to see the ghost of Thomas Holcomb, gun in his hand.

The shadow from the woods stood by his side.

***

Emelda could barely see now.

María Martin's sharp smile cut into her, the face of someone who reveled in their cruelty but even more in their gloating honesty.

William was dead.

"I understand he fought to get back to you," María added. "You know he killed my man Antonio? Bashed his head in with a rock, if you can believe such a thing. I always knew William was a killer; from the moment we met I could smell the violence on him."

There was so much Emelda wanted to say. She wanted to curse, to scream. To fall to her knees and weep. She wanted to claw out her eyes, tear at her hair. But instead she was motionless. It was hard to breathe, so impossibly hard. Instead of words only absurd clicking sounds escaped her throat.

"I never lied to him. Or to you," María added. "I thought of William like a son. His friendship meant the world to me, infected by socialism though he was. And you…well, I always saw myself in you, Emelda. So very smart, driven. Kind."

"You're not *kind*!" The words escaped Emelda's mouth in a high-pitched scream. "Stop it. Stop it with this fucking comic-book villain *bullshit*! You killed my husband, what did you do to my *son*? Where is my *baby*?"

The sharp edges of María's smile softened. She set down her cup of tea.

The portrait of Elizabeth Holcomb seemed tired behind her.

"I didn't kill your husband, Emelda. I could never. And though you won't believe me, I'm sorry for what is happening to you. I know firsthand that no mother should have to outlive all her children."

"Shut up, shut up!" Emelda screamed back. "Just tell me what you've done with Christopher. Just tell me and kill me. Leave my family alone!"

"The children in the forest." María turned away from Emelda and towards the window. In the dark a few glowing bodies could be seen, watching carefully as more and more shadows walked into the yards and gardens of Casa Verde.

"After Holcomb's covenant with the nation, a select few of the people of Rio Rojo realized the same thing their ancestors had before them. The devil's cradle has never been conquered, never been subdued. The Rio Sangria cuts this land deep with red water, Emelda. It gives it life, and in turn we gave it life too."

When she turned back to Emelda, there was water in her eyes.

"It was horrible, watching my youngest drown in that river. But watching him rise up…I tell you, there is no greater joy in realizing that your child can *never* die."

She stepped forward and placed Emelda's hands in hers. She looked her in the eyes, almost tenderly.

"My little boy doesn't hurt anymore, Emelda. All the nation

asks for is their last little breaths, and in return it gives us so much. Power. Security. And *beautiful* little children, who will never die again.

"But your son is different, Emelda. You must have realized the moment you gave birth to him how different he was. Holcomb made his covenant with Antioch, and Antioch made Thomas Holcomb. He became its vessel, and it became his familiar. A shadow, which only left his side after he passed."

Whatever kindness, humanity was left contorted into an expression of zeal, of dark rapture. The lines across María Martin's face were pulled tight, a leathery, monstrous expression of glee.

"We have renewed our covenant: we have made our offer to the nation. And it has chosen your son."

There was an explosion outside. A bright light made the night look like day. The sky was brilliant blue, the forest bright and vibrant green. The earth shook beneath them. María screamed as she was knocked off her feet.

Emelda crouched down.

The screech of a second mortar howled through the air. The splinter of trees in thousands of burning embers followed. Casa Verde shook, an old home trembling in the fire.

"No." María gritted her teeth.

Emelda remained frozen, waiting as the sound of a low-flying plane came from above.

"No!" María shrieked. "That bastard moved *first*! He *lied*!"

María looked back out the window.

Emelda stood up and crept behind her.

Rio Rojo was on fire. In the light she could make out the navy's river boats firing from the red water. Small airplanes circled in the sky, sweeping down low to pour lightning strikes of bullets down on the town. Armored vehicles were moving slowly up the hill, through the streets.

The gunfire was definitive. The warning bells of her story's final arc.

"That evil bastard planned to invade the moment he met me!" María shrieked. "It was never about taking Margería, it was about meeting me here! Well, I'll meet him. I've already made my offer to the nation! It's already been accepted! I'll—"

Emelda used her entire weight to shove María Martin through the window. María only had time for one gasp before her body shattered the window. Glass poured like heavy rain, glinting orange in the air with reflected fire. The old woman fell quietly, but landed loudly on the wooden porch. Emelda only looked once.

Her body was twisted and ruined. Blood seeped into her black dress. But there was no mistaking her face.

Emelda raced down the stairs, calling out for her children.

***

Edward only saw the shadow, the ghost of Holcomb, once before the sky was set on fire.

The bomb cut into the hills around them, scattering a wave of dirt, smoke, and ash. Awakened by the fury, the birds flew into the air, panicked. Other animals stirred from their rest, running headlong from the woods and into the open gardens. The armed men and women around Casa Verde shouted in surprise, taking their arms meekly up to the sky.

In the light of the fires, Edward could make out another face lying just beneath Holcomb's likeness.

The shadow at his brother's side roared, as if in pain or anger.

But Christopher didn't balk, didn't move. He only stood still for a moment, before resuming his slow, careful walk.

Edward didn't look back again. "Come on!" he cried out to

his sisters.

Running into the woods was the only way. The soldiers would come to Casa Verde first. There would be places to hide along the river, to wait out the storms of fire and bullets. And the expression in his brother's face was one he had never seen before.

Torie and Téa panted behind him. He could hear them screaming as behind them clouds of flames puffed up like orange flower blossoms. Somewhere in the town, someone was ringing the church bell, a funeral dirge for a fiery mass grave.

But a shot rang out just behind them.

Téa fell. In the fires Edward could see the dark blood pouring from her arm. She cried, almost screamed at the sight. Above his sister's wailing, he reached for the gun at his side.

But he'd given it away.

Torie shot back at her brother. "Go!" she shouted. She wasn't running. His stomach fell when he remembered. He never made her *promise* to run.

Edward stopped.

Her feet were parted apart, her back was straight. Just like Father had taught them.

"Take care of Téa and go!"

"I—"

"You're a great big brother. The best. She's going to need you for what comes next."

Something took over him. A cold, mechanical thoughtlessness. He lifted his little sister up, a screaming, crying doll in his arms. The thoughtlessness made him strong, so she was light in his arms. It made him fast, faster than he had ever been before.

But it couldn't stop him from crying.

***

Torie wasn't scared of the dark anymore.

She wasn't scared of the shadow that clung to Christopher, or of the gun in her brother's arms. She was scared that she wouldn't be able to slow him down long enough for Edward and Téa to get away. And that fear kept her ready, kept her resolute.

The shadow roared from beside Christopher, growling low like a hungry jungle cat. Its yellow eyes fixated on her, and she felt the same sensation of being small that she had when she first saw it.

But she wasn't so small anymore.

"Christopher," she whispered.

But the thing wearing her brother's face didn't respond.

"You took my brother!" she yelled at the shadow.

The shadow stood in silence, as if to confirm what she said.

Around her the world kept burning. There were screams coming from Rio Rojo, crying from the throats of horrified mothers clutching their bleeding children. Tears from old men, wondering how they could still be alive after witnessing so much carnage and death.

She kept her pistol trained on her brother's chest.

Father had said to fire at a man's torso. The largest part of his body.

Christopher, or the thing that held his body, raised his rifle too.

There had been a time when she was afraid. Of bugs. Of thunder. When she would weep uncontrollably and run to Edward's room. Edward would always console her. Edward had always been there.

He'd be there.

She'd make sure of it.

Torie closed her eyes and fired.

Her brother fired back.

The pain in her stomach was unlike any other. She opened her eyes. She dropped the pistol. Instinctively, her hands went to her stomach. How much blood could there be inside her?

She fell to the ground.

Her brother's rifle kissed her head.

***

The people ransacking Casa Verde were now running towards the town. The small army had turned its attention away from the Esquival family and towards the sudden, unexpected invasion of their town.

Emelda ran over the scattered papers, leapt across overturned tables and chairs.

"Edward! Victoria!" All the doors were open. The death squads had been searching for them. "Kids!"

They were smart. They would hide, they would run.

"Kids, please, it's me! We need to leave!"

But no one answered her back. She ran between the rooms, terrified that she would find their bleeding, open bodies.

"Please!" she screamed.

The back door was open.

They would run.

"Kids!"

Her life didn't matter anymore. She could die, and nothing would change. She would be with William again. She desperately believed in heaven now, with a furor she never had before. There had to be a life after this one, where she could lean against her husband, where she could hold him in her arms and where he could hold her back. She could die now. But she needed to protect them. Needed to find them.

The door to the back gardens was open.

"Kids!"

Trees were burning now. The gardens seemed massive, standing dark against the dim orange flames.

But through the fire, she recognized the outline of a boy with long, curly hair.

"Christopher!" she called out.

She ran to him, faster than she had ever done before.

Her son ignored her.

"Christopher!" But he kept walking away.

There was something on the ground.

Victoria's head was wide and open. Her stomach was red and wet.

"W-what?"

Emelda always thought the name "Victoria" was beautiful. Always insisted on calling her little girl by her full name.

Why was her little girl so pale? Why was she asleep out here?

"Torie."

Why was she so cold to the touch? Why was there blood on her dress?

"Torie?"

Emelda couldn't think. She couldn't feel the ground beneath her. What was this thing that looked so much like her daughter's corpse?

There was a pistol at Torie's side. Emelda took it in her hands.

"Christopher!"

Finally, her son turned to face her.

His hair was brown now. His eyes were shining green. Behind him stood a cloud of darkness, a swirling with hungry green eyes.

"What have you done!?"

But her son was buried beneath whatever thing had taken over him.

He raised his rifle towards her.

And she fired once.

The bullet struck his shoulder. He dropped his rifle.

She ran forward.

The shadow snarled at her, but she wouldn't let it have him. Not her boy. Not her baby.

The nation had taken so much from her. She wouldn't let it take any more.

Her hands pressed down on her son's neck. Her knees pressed down on his chest. Her thumbs dug deep. Her teeth bit into each other. Every part of her body and soul howled.

Her son's eyes rolled back, and she could see their normal brown return.

María had said he was gone. But before her eyes, he was coming back. His dark hair. His kind face.

The shadow howled in pain beside them, but it didn't matter. What mattered was the thing inside her son getting strangled away. That it left him with her. That it let her keep him.

Her wrists tightened. Her son's body kicked wildly. She didn't feel his scratches, the cuts along her arms. She only felt his heartbeat. Slowing. Fading.

His arms stopped thrashing. His legs stopped kicking.

The shadow's howling became whimpers.

Her son's eyes turned brown.

Emelda smiled. "Christopher!"

But he wouldn't answer.

She placed a hand to his face.

Where was he?

Where was his smile?

Where was her *favorite smile*?

***

Edward ran as long as he could before his legs and heart finally gave out. His blood pounded in his ears, and every breath cut his throat. Téa couldn't stop crying, and neither could he. He cradled his little sister close to him, hugged her so tight that it must have hurt both of them.

They hid beneath the bushes, whimpering like puppies in the cold.

Christopher had killed Torie. He would have killed them too, but his bullet only grazed Téa's arm.

She'd wanted him to be a big brother to Téa, but she didn't realize how special she was. How could he be the same big brother to Téa when Téa wasn't her? He wanted to run back, to fight off whatever shadow had wrapped itself around Christopher, and save his sister. But the two gunshots he'd heard in the distance told him all he needed to know.

Torie was gone. And Christopher could still be hunting them.

The children of the forest came to them slowly, slinking out from beneath the trees and branches. Their dark smiles were sad, even kind. They came closer now, sitting beside them.

"We're sorry," a young girl said.

If he looked at her just right, she seemed like Torie. With her dark hair. With no eyes, he may as well imagine Torie's, glimmering in the night.

"This happened to all of us, you know?"

"We all died once," a little boy said. "It only hurt once. And now we never hurt again."

Edward had been hurting for what seemed like so long. He was tired in a way he never knew he could be.

"The army is coming," he told the children.

"Yes," the little girl with short black hair said. "They'll be here at any moment."

"I don't know what they'll do with me. Or my sister."

"Neither do we. But"—she smiled earnestly now—"you could stay here. You could be one of us. And you'd never get hurt. You'd never get tired."

He shook his head. "No, no, I don't want to die."

"It's so much easier than living, though!" she responded with such childlike enthusiasm and earnestness.

"Even if that's true…no. There's someone more important than me now, and I've got to be there for them."

"There's a lot more important people than you, Edward Esquival II."

The girl from the house, with short hair and brilliant blue eyes, wore an expression of pure rage on her face. Her face was red, her teeth bared and sharp. Her rifle was trained on his head.

"Your whore mother killed Christopher! Killed the one hope this nation had!" She clutched her stomach. "Even if Holcomb's blood is still here it's not enough! Do you understand!? We need a living ancestor to lead us now!"

"I—"

"No, Edward Esquival. Your father couldn't talk his way out of this, and neither can you! We're going down to the river. You're going to do what you must for this country! Or I will shoot you here and now, and I will splatter that pretty little girl's head all over this goddamn forest! Do you understand?"

Edward pulled Téa close to him. He couldn't do it. He couldn't let her die. "You'll protect her? If I go?"

"If you do exactly what I say, and if you lead us, I will die to protect your little sister. I promise."

"How do I know I can believe you?"

"I am many things, Edward. But I am no liar. Your brother knew that."

"Are you Alma Sales?"

"I am."

"Did…did you love Christopher? Really?"

"More than you'll ever know."

Edward thought. He looked at Téa. She looked up at him, her face wet and red. The bullet was still in her arm.

"Clean her wound," he told the girl with the gun. "Clean her wound, take care of her, and I'll go with you. I'll do whatever you want."

"Good boy." Alma smiled. She bent down to Téa, and put her fingers in the wound. Téa winced and screamed. Then Alma poured water over the blood and bound her shoulder tight with cloth she ripped from the sleeves of her uniform.

Téa was crying again when Alma gingerly placed her beneath a tree. "The children will stay with her, and they won't hurt her. We can go."

Edward turned to Téa and knelt down in front of her. She wouldn't look at him when he ran his hands through her hair. "It's not fair to you, Téa. But you're going to have to be strong for all of us now."

"No…Eddie, no!" she whimpered.

"It's like you said earlier. We're all brave. And I'm so sorry. You're going to have to be the bravest."

"No…please don't leave me! Don't go die!"

"I'll be right back. Wait for Mom. If she doesn't come, wait for a soldier. Tell them you're lost. Tell them you're an orphan. Lie about your name."

"No, Eddie!"

"I love you, little sister. I just wish I said that more."

He stood up. Alma still had her gun trained on him. He looked around to the children still glowing in the night. "Will you watch her for me? Until I come back."

They nodded.

He held his hand out to Alma. "I know it's silly…but will you hold my hand? I'm not going to run away, but I'm still scared."

Alma laughed softly. "Sure. Let's go."

As they walked away, Téa was still screaming out for him.

***

Téa couldn't stop crying this time.

The woods were dark, and she no longer liked the children who clung so close to her. She knew what they were now, and it finally scared her. She wanted Daddy, Mommy. Wanted Christopher to stop hunting them.

The girl with the gun had said Christopher was dead. Was Torie dead too? Why?

She pulled herself into her knees. She hated it here. She wanted to go back to when Daddy would cook bacon and eggs on Sunday mornings. When Mommy would tease him about putting sugar in his coffee, and he would smile and make some joke that made her groan. She wanted to go back to when Christopher would just roll his eyes and grin even though he didn't like the joke, and when Edward and Torie would sit quietly and eat, just happy to be with each other.

There had been a time before all of this. Before the people with guns, the ghosts and the shadows that wanted to destroy them. A time before the fire and the army. When Daddy would receive visitors and Mommy would call them by their first names. When even Téa could play with other kids in the city, kids she'd called her friends, though now she couldn't even remember their faces.

The children tried to reassure her, but their touch was too cold and too smooth. She winced and wailed, throwing herself away from them. Why did they have to be here? Why couldn't the big girl have just left them alone?

Alone.

She was alone now.

But she didn't know how to find her way in the dark. How to fight for herself. How was she going to survive?

Wait, Edward had said. For the army. Lie about her name.

But 'Téa' was the only name she ever knew.

She thought of something else. What other name would she want to call herself? She'd always thought 'Victoria' was very pretty.

She couldn't stop crying now. She was loud, so loud. The soldiers would find her. Someone or something would find her.

The children tried to shush her again, but it only made her cry louder.

Téa heard footsteps coming through the woods. She put both hands over her mouth and tried to hide in the hollow of a tree. Her breathing was fluttering and ragged.

The figure walking through the forest was tall and held a gun in its hands. It had long, tangled hair and seemed to stop only every now and then to scan the ground.

For a long time, the whole world stopped making noise. Téa even tried to stop breathing.

"Téa? Is that you?"

"Mommy!"

Téa ran out from the tree hollow. The children were gone. The woods were gone.

Her mother stood with her arms outstretched. She threw herself into her mother and wept. Mommy's arms seemed so strong, so much stronger than any monster.

"Téa," Mother asked, "where is your brother?"

***

Edward walked with his hand in Alma Sales's for what seemed like half an hour. In that time he kept quiet, to himself. He tried to will himself into having peaceful final moments, spending time only with the memories he liked the most. Torie giving him a Christmas card she drew herself. Father teaching him how to fish. Mother teaching him to read. Riding bikes through Margería, trying to keep up as Christopher flew ahead of him.

He tried to ignore the shadow that walked with him, the one that had walked with Christopher before.

But Alma Sales wouldn't let him. "Do you recognize it, Edward? Do you see it for what it is?"

"No," he replied.

Her smile widened. "That's *Antioch*, that's the whole nation, walking beside you."

He didn't understand. For all he knew, Alma was insane. It could be nonsense, ravings. But there would be no escaping it.

"We'll offer you to the nation," Alma continued. "And the nation will accept you. Gardner may be making his own offer, a better offer, but you have Holcomb's blood in you. The nation's first and favorite son!

"I know you must be scared, but you're in your seat of power. Do not be afraid."

Antonio's words to him in the library came back to him. *Your seat of power.*

Every part of this was inevitable. They were always going to die here. But the army's sudden attack had surprised their killers. Not thwarted them, just merely disrupted them.

"Can I tell you something?" he asked Alma.

"Of course."

"I don't think a cruel country is worth this. I don't want to die for a cruel nation."

"But you're going to anyway."

"But I'm going to anyway," he conceded.

"Heh."

They came to the shore of the Rio Sangria.

Elizabeth Holcomb stood tall and pale in the water. Her eyes swirled black, and her arms were as wide as the sky. A chill came from her, waving across the water and freezing him in his path.

"Go to her," Alma growled.

But she was the most frightening thing he had ever seen.

A gun cocked behind him.

"I know this forest like the back of my hand. I know *exactly* where I left your little sister, and I will go back and I will fucking kill her if you do not go to her!"

The shadow roared and snarled beside her.

Edward slowly stepped into the water. It was colder than it had been the day before, as if jagged chunks of ice instead of rock were sliding along the soles of his shoes.

Elizabeth loomed over him. Her smile was bright in the night, the soft smile of a mother trying to calm a frightened child.

She would take him in her arms, and he would go down into the water with her. Down and down. He wouldn't breathe again. And whatever came up, it wouldn't be him.

He remembered what the children had said.

He wouldn't hurt. Not ever again.

He tried to smile.

"No!"

A gunshot rang out. On the shore, Alma Sales only wavered for a moment before falling to the rocks. Emelda stood with her feet apart, pistol still smoking in her hands. Alma bled out profusely from her ruined head. The shadow's roaring was louder than the gunshots, than the explosions.

"No!" Emelda roared back. She stood defiantly, shoulders forward as she screamed at the nation. "You *can't have him*! He's *mine*!"

Elizabeth waded forward, swimming towards him.

"Eddie!"

He moved forward, running back towards the shore. The water made him slow, lapping at his knees and pulling him along the riverbed.

A cold hand grabbed his ankles and pulled him back.

Emelda ran into the water. His mother's warm hands latched onto his wrists.

"You can't have him!"

He felt like he was going to be pulled apart, but he kicked furiously. "Mom!"

"You *can't have him!*"

Fire rose above the trees. Gunshots filled the air, and with them the shouting of soldiers.

The hands at his ankles let go. His mother pulled him to shore. She held him, wet and sopping. They breathed heavily, desperately.

Edward turned once to Elizabeth. She stood still in the water, a look of utter heartbreak on her face.

The shadow seemed to shrink the fire.

"You there!"

The soldiers burst through the trees, the flag of Antioch on their shoulders. Their arms raised, they lowered when they met a woman holding her child. "Ma'am, are you okay? Who are you?"

Emelda was quiet.

"Ma'am."

Edward remembered what his mother had said. He stood up and held up his arms.

"My name is Edgar Sepulveda! Please, my mother and little sister have been waiting for the army! They killed my father, my brother, my sister! Please help us!"

Emelda looked at her son for a moment, as if somewhere far away. Then she ran forward, throwing herself at the feet of the soldiers. "Please, please help us!"

***

Declaration from the Honorable Colonel Gardner and the Military Junta.

Countrymen, last night the armed forces launched a surprise operation in Rio Rojo. There, they discovered the presence of communist rebels, as well as separatist terrorists from Rio Rojo. Casa Verde, the ancestral home of Thomas Holcomb, has been burnt to the ground.

As the night before was, last night was difficult. In the coming days we will learn more about the innocent citizens slaughtered by the terrorists, but we must thank our heroes in the armed forces for saving those who they could. Survivors from Rio Rojo are currently making their way across the country to new homes, as the town is rebuilt by the armed forces.

President Ambert would be proud of you all, and I am proud to call you my brothers, my father, my sisters and mother. Antioch has been through dark night after dark night, but I promise there will be better days ahead.

For the glory of Antioch,
Colonel Gardner

EPILOGUE:

Emelda held her daughter in her lap.

Téa wouldn't stop growing, despite the world's best efforts. But now as she slept deeply, Emelda treasured how small she still was. She still wore a red ribbon in her hair, and at the sight of it, Emelda could not help but remember her husband.

The boat was full of people from across Antioch, people who were going to find a home abroad. The ambassadors of various nations had appealed directly to Colonel Gardner to allow people with dual citizenship to return to their various countries of origin.

Emelda suspected that everyone on the boat was leaving bodies behind. She would never know where William was buried. Her daughter would have no gravestone. And Christopher...

She could not let herself remember her eldest.

Not now.

It had been difficult, but Emelda had found someone who could forge passports. It took leaving Rio Rojo for a small coastal town, a place where the flood of the coup's changes had been slow to travel. She hadn't had much, but some mix of the wadded bills she still had and the desperate child in her arms moved the forger's sympathy as well as his greed.

She did not like the name 'Sepulveda,' but once abroad, she could declare herself for who she was. Emelda had friends across the world, and she would find them. She would never speak ill of Gardner, though. She would not raise the alarm, would cause no spies to come after her.

She was content with having her small world. Little Téa and Edward. If Gardner would let her keep them, she would never say a word against him.

Edward was wide awake, watching the different passengers and listening intently to the languages they spoke. The boat was enormous, a repurposed cruise ship. But they were sitting on the top deck, looking at the sunlight and watching Antioch fade away one last time.

The coastal town had been quiet and uneventful, but humid

and hot. In the distance its neat white buildings and colorful banners grew smaller.

There was a limit on the plundered money and artifacts from Casa Verde Emelda would be able to sell discreetly, but she'd bought their way onto this ship. She would keep fighting, as she always did. They would survive; they would do whatever it was that they needed to.

Edward held her hand. Emelda smiled and brought it to her lips.

"We're going to be okay," she whispered. "One day, we're going to be okay."

"I know," he said.

He had been pretending to be brave and strong. Maybe that was part of it, though, keeping a strong face even though you were hurting. Emelda didn't want that for him. When they were safe, they would cry again, but then they would laugh. Vivid memories of her husband's murder would be overtaken by memories of long mornings in bed. The smell of him. The kindness and strength of him.

Edward and Téa would grow old, and she would do whatever she could to make sure they grew happy. They would tell stories about Christopher and Torie. Funny stories. Sad stories. Stories that would make them laugh until they cried, and stories that made them cry until they laughed.

She was taking her inspiration from them, and trying to be strong. Some nights though she would wake to screaming, and search wildly to wake Torie from one of her night terrors. Darting about in the dark for her daughter, Emelda always remembered that the screams, and the terrors, were only her own. And the ocean outside, its current pouring into the mouth of a river that ran red miles away, would respond with a quiet lapping sounding like muffled laughter.

One day, she might let herself rest. One day, she might tell Edward about María Martin.

About Christopher.

But for now, all she could do was swallow to keep from crying.

"Your father would be so proud of you," she said as the seagulls flew overhead and the salt filled the air. "He was always proud of you."

"Do you think we can come back one day?" he finally asked. "To put him in a better grave? To put all of them in better graves?"

"I...I don't know, honey. But what I do know is that as long as we're alive, that's what's important. That's what would make them happy."

At this, he was quiet again.

As Antioch faded away, they could faintly make out the mouth of Rio Sangria. At its mouth, the river was just as blue in the ocean, but glittered bright pink-scarlet under the setting sun. And between the shimmers of sunlight, Emelda saw the pale shapes of what could be glistening bodies.

AUTHOR'S AFTERWORD

What sort of nation is Antioch?

I should explain myself. In March 2020, I was on board one of the last commercial flights out of Bogotá, Colombia. I had been conducting academic research, and had spent three months in Colombia's capital.

Colombia is, in many senses, an exceptional nation. But then, all nations are "exceptional." There is an eagerness, though, to simplify a nation's exceptionalism by its best and worst stories. And to understand both stories from Colombia, you need to understand its geography:

Colombia is at the top of the South American continent. It has coasts on the Pacific and the Atlantic, and is connected to North America via the narrow strip of land called "Panama" which it once owned. It has some of the most fertile soil in the world, and some of the most difficult geography too. There are gentle, warm places to be sure. But not Bogotá. Bogotá is unusually cold, more like Seattle than Medellín or Cartagena. It's grey. It rains. Every day I would try to run home before the storms, and I spent money on *multiple* umbrellas.

So readers could be forgiven for thinking that Antioch is merely a fictional stand-in for Colombia, which after all found itself cursed with plentiful resources and a geographic location that would make it a critical waypoint in the various corridors of power networked across the Americas. But to assign Antioch the status of a fictional analog is dangerous, misleading and in fact not my intent.

I have studied and lived in Latin America, and many readers in the past have commented that I am producing "Latin American" stories or "Latin American horror." I am not, for many reasons. The foremost being that I am not Latin American.

But there is an impulse in horror to ascribe terror to 'the other.' 'The unknown.'

Antioch must be some distant country then. Because it is an 'other.' The things that happen in Antioch, in this story, they don't happen here.

Except when they do.

This novel was written over the long pandemic, when I was convinced I would never have a chance to write a novel again. It was written on weekends, in eight-hour shifts, with the guiding question of "What would I like to read next if I was the reader" leading to a short, brutal story of a family swallowed whole by a national collapse. National collapses don't happen here. Except when they do.

On January 6th, 2021, an armed mob sieged the US Capitol.

Jake Tapper on CNN, commented: "This is like watching a scene from Bogotá."

Except armed insurgents hadn't had a major presence in the city for twenty years.

Perhaps Mr. Tapper was thinking of "the Bogotazo," a riot which caused a collapse of the national government and whipped Colombia's partisan factions into a civil war. Except that those happened in 1948, well before Mr. Tapper was born. And the Colombian press responded in kind, calling the siege on the United States' Capitol "the Washingtanazo."

What sort of nation is Antioch?

Antioch is the United States, where even saying the words "January 6th" is now interpreted as the utterance of a partisan declaration rather than the invocation of a vivid, horrible memory. Antioch is France, where religious and political factionalism spurred a nationalist conqueror who would spread his own wars throughout Europe. Antioch is European, locked in a region known for political intrigue, nationalism. A place of continental wars and the cradle of both world wars.

What sort of nation is Antioch?

It's not an 'other.' But it is 'exceptional.'

Antioch is the same thing that all nations are. A lesson, a story, and a cautionary fable.

—S. L. Edwards, 4/8/2022

ACKNOWLEDGEMENTS

The obvious person to begin with is Scarlett Algee.

This novel was written in what was, for me, absolute worst period of the pandemic. My first collection *Whiskey and Other Unusual Ghosts* went out of print, and I'd hit a wall with my writing. This, compounded with the extreme isolation and the lingering feeling that we were living through the slow end of the world made me more bitter and hostile to writing and writers than I have ever been before or since.

Scarlett saved this novel, rescued it from its writer.

Then of course there's Ross E. Lockhart, who read the first section and told me to keep going. Yves Tourigny, who contributed some of his best work yet to the cover. I know we shouldn't judge books by their covers, but he portrayed Casa Verde and Rio Rojo with so much latent dread.

Then there are the other writers. Brian Evenson was incredibly encouraging in this endeavor and was one of the novel's biggest advocates before it was even written. John Langan too, seemed interested and ready for the novel as it was being written. Justin Burnett was the first or second beta reader and gave brilliant feedback. S.P. Miskowski, Todd Keisling, Carson Winters, Peter Rawlik and Laird Barron contributed some very kind words for the novel, and I hope the book in your hands meets their praise.

I'm not sure if this work would be in your hands at all if it wasn't for someone like Nadia Bulkin, who really should be credited with pioneering the way politics and partisanship are portrayed in ghost stories. Peter Straub's *Ghost Story* and Richard Matheson's *Hell House* were both influences too, Matheson more than Straub. Outside of horror, I'd be remiss to not nod to Boris Pasternak and Vasily Grossman, whose portrayal of war as horror left a huge impression on me.

My friends who are fellow creatives also encouraged this thing to move forward. KA Opperman and Ashley Dioses, Matthew M. Bartlett, John Linwood Grant, John Paul Fitch, Russell Smeaton, Brooklyne Warra, Gwendolyn Kiste, Jon Padgett, William Tea. This book would not exist without you all.

And then there's grandmama, whose stories connected me to all the family who I never knew. She looms over the Esquivals, a living matriarch and a pillar of my own life. I love you, grandmama.

—S. L. Edwards 9/7/2022

ABOUT THE AUTHOR

S. L. Edwards is a world-travelling Texan finally headed home. He enjoys dark fiction, dark poetry and darker beer. His debut short story collection, *Whiskey and Other Unusual Ghosts* is being re-released by Journalstone, who published his second collection, *The Death of An Author*. *In the Devil's Cradle* is his first novel.

www.ingramcontent.com/pod-product-compliance
Lightning Source LLC
Chambersburg PA
CBHW031058020726
47495CB00007B/1939